REDEMPTION

Legends of Graham Mansion
Book One

Rosa Lee Jude

Rosa Lee Jude

Mary Lin Brewer

Mary Lin Brewer

This is a work of fiction.

All of the characters, organizations, and events portrayed in this novel

are either products of the authors' imaginations

or are used as fictional characters.

DEDICATION

To the man who saved the Mansion
Josiah Cephas Weaver

The Keys to Our Success

It's a brave thing to hand over your dream to another person. I thank Mary Lin for allowing me to take her vision, be the surrogate mother, and add my own spin. It's a rare opportunity to take a piece of history and make it your own.

I have been fortunate to have some wonderful people in my life. It began with parents who encouraged reading, learning and striving for excellence. It's continued with friends who cheer me on no matter what crazy thing I am currently doing. Two of these friends have had a key role in this journey: my first writing partner and kindred spirit – Pam Newberry – and the most prolific reader I know, my soul sister – Marcella Taylor.

We all need someone in our lives who just lets us be ourselves. No matter what new adventure that I pursue, professionally or personally, my patient and compassionate husband, Ron, does not question or criticize my dreams. After 20 years of practice, he simply lets me be me. He is a true blessing in my life.

Lastly, I thank the fuzziest member of our family, Princess Mia, for loyally sitting by my side during the long hours at the keyboard.

~ Rosa Lee Jude

It was my mother, Mary Grace Queen Megginson, the quintessential journalist, who taught me to love reading, writing, and most of all, the sheer power of words. I love you, Mom. It is the blessing of my life to have been raised by parents who modeled and demanded hard work, life-long learning, and loyalty.

I first saw the Mansion in 2004 when Josiah Cephas Weaver opened that massive medieval-looking front door. Even now, I sometimes have to remember to breathe there. Thank you, Josiah.

It happened back in 2006 as I awaited the grim prognosis of my almost-flat tire at Atkins Tire Company in Wytheville, Virginia. As the owner pulled out a wayward nail and patched the hole, he announced out of the clear blue, "You know my wife comes from that Joseph Baker family...the one who was killed by his slaves." And that is how I met Jo Carol Atkins. She and an army of Baker descendants have guarded and passed down the Baker genealogy, family portraits, and letters since the 1600s. Local historian, middle school teacher, and Graham descendant, Davy Davis, did much of the deep research which helped us to hobble together the limited facts surrounding Joseph Baker's life...and untimely death. Thank you, Davy, and thanks to all of the Baker descendants who have provided these missing pieces.

I met Rosa some five years ago. She was leading a regional tourism conference and I sat down in her room by mistake. She began to talk before I could sneak out. Then, she said more in two minutes that directly related to my woeful music festival than all the experts I had listened to (and paid) for two years. I did not know then that she was a writer. I know now. Thanks, Rosa. Hard work, learning, and loyalty...it is indeed a divine sisterhood.

~ Mary Lin Brewer

There are so few people in the world who know us both and the subject well enough to create a perfect trifecta, yet Tami Quinn accomplished that feat. Thank you, Tami, for connecting us.

Who would take our words and handle them with care and save us from ourselves? That would be our Editor, Donna Stroupe. Thanks for seeing everything wrong and everything right and for loving our story almost as much as we did.

Thank you to our graphic designer, Robin Lewis, for creating the cover of our dreams.

Our utmost thanks to all of the above and to all those others who have inspired and empowered us. And most of all, our gratitude goes to all those who will read these pages and travel with us to another time.

~ Rosa Lee Jude & Mary Lin Brewer

The Story Behind The Story

The *Legends of Graham Mansion* series was the dream of Mary Lin Brewer. After almost a decade of hearing countless stories about the Major Graham Mansion property from descendants of the Graham and Baker families, neighbors, historians, and friends, Mary Lin longed for the creation of a series of books that would give a fictionalized look at the property's long history. Sometimes, history doesn't tell a good story and she wanted something written that would entertain and encourage people to want to learn more.

She had the idea for a central heroine of the series and that this young character would travel through time to discover the mysteries and secrets from the lives of the many generations who had lived on the property. But her strengths were not in creative writing, she was more of a researcher by nature. So she found a writer who could spin a yarn and create a world and story around her idea. She found a kindred spirit who could make the history interesting. That writer was Rosa Lee Jude. A collaboration was soon formed. Mary Lin would provide the research, history and access to the property and Rosa Lee would help bring Mary Lin's dream to life and add a few dreams of her own.

Redemption is the first installment in the *Legends of Graham Mansion* series. The core historical aspect focuses on the family that is believed to be the property's first non-Native American residents, the Bakers. Joseph Joel Baker, his wife Nannie, their children and slaves lived on the property in log cabins in the latter 1700s. He was a distiller, farmer, and had served in the militia. Court records relate that Joseph Baker was murdered by two of his slaves, Bob and Sam, in May, 1786. They were tried and hung for this crime. Few other facts are known about the incident or the family.

This is a work of historical fiction. History has been used in the creation of this story, but the majority of what will be found within these pages is pure fiction, a speculative look at what might have occurred. The authors have endeavored to be true to the time period and respectful to those real persons who are fictionally portrayed. The story also has the twist of time travel and a glimmer of paranormal. The later aspects are due, in part, to some of the accounts that the many ghost hunters, clairvoyants, and paranormal experts have relayed to Mary Lin in recent years.

Major Graham Mansion is a very real place. It is located in Wythe County in the beautiful Blue Ridge Mountains of Southwest Virginia just a few miles from the historic Great Wagon Road and the New River as well as modern-day interstates I-77 and I-81. The property has been owned, renovated, and maintained for over 20 years by Virginia native, Josiah Cephas Weaver. The Mansion is open seasonally for a variety of special events, haunted history tours, paranormal investigations, and the widely popular event, SpookyWorld.

PRESENT DAY

ONE

Tap, tap, tap, a cold March rain pelted the old cobalt blue and clear glass window panes. Grae's mood matched the weather - dreary, sullen, and dark. She was a classic seventeen-year-old girl in all the outward ways, but inside revealed a secret self, a girl longing for adventure. She sat curled up in a ball on the window seat, arms encircling her legs, head tilted to the left and resting on her knees as she gazed out at the fog. It was her "safe ball" position as her brother Perry called it.

Since moving to Virginia the previous fall, Grae had spent a lot of time sitting in the room of glass, as she deemed it. It wasn't a move that she wanted to make; she'd left the only life she'd ever known in the midst of her senior year of high school. From a suburb of Charlotte, North Carolina, to a small town in the Blue Ridge Mountains, the change was dramatic, but it had to be.

Her emotionally distant father had used creative accounting to deceive a legion of his investment firm's clients and amassed a double life for himself. He'd conned his family as well into believing his visionary investment strategy was making everyone wealthy. He didn't envision that the FBI and the Securities and Exchange Commission would learn of his exceptional abilities and take exception with him. The Enron scandal had taken away the possibility of just a warning and probation. White collar criminals could now expect tougher prosecutors, sterner judges, and harsher sentences. All their assets were seized and sold to pay off his debts. Ten days after the bars of a federal prison cell in Butner, North Carolina, closed behind Grae's father, her mother slammed the back door of a U-Haul truck on all they had left of their previous life, and the journey began.

Her mother, Mary Katherine, "Kat," brought them to her hometown in Virginia. It was a move designed by shear need. Their gilded suburban life was gone and all the luxuries with it. No more two-story colonial on a cul-de-sac or playing golf and tennis at the country club. No more designer name clothes for Grae, or personal archery lessons for Perry. Tom White shot a bull's eye through that life, and left three survivors.

Now a middle-aged housewife returning home in her aging Jeep, Kat lamented not keeping in touch with at least a few hometown friends and regretted the promising career she gave up in finance. It was the love of her life, Tom, now Prisoner No. 61726-054, who craved the perfect family, the stay-at-home wife persona. Kat gave him that, along with a piece of her soul. So, with no money, no possessions, no recent work history, and two teenagers, Kat went home. Back to a world she never thought she would return to, but which gave her comfort in her desperate situation.

Grae's grandmother, Belle, died the previous year after an early stroke took her mobility and her dignity, but not her sense of sarcastic humor. That sarcasm gene was passed to Grae, much to the aggravation of her mother. Grae's grandfather, Peirce, "Mack," had been the caretaker of Major Graham Mansion since he retired a dozen years earlier. Age never slowed him down, but his dear Belle's death made him an old man. After her passing, he rented out their lifelong home and moved himself into the Mansion to escape the pain of the present by attempting to preserve the past.

The Mansion was a massive place. The original structure was built in the 1830s with additions made a few decades later that brought it to its current 11-room, 11,000-square foot size. Each room on both the first and second floors seemed to have a life of its own. While the walls and their décor had changed through the decades of the house's life, the majority of the floors, doorframes and trimmings were original, as were the Mansion's tall windows. Legend said that a local door tax charged a tax payer by the door, so the floor-to-ceiling windows throughout the Mansion helped to ease that burden.

Summers spent as a caretaker's helper while in his teens gave Mack a sentimental perspective to his duties and some incredible stories about its history. The owner worshipped Mack and depended on him to take the lead in preservation and needed repairs. Even though it had been almost half a century since it had been used as a residence, he was given permission to move his daughter and grandchildren into the Mansion when they needed a place to live.

And that was where Grae found herself on that rainy March day - in a big old drafty mansion with a history as old as the country she lived in, but a world apart from anything she had previously known. Grae was grateful that the owner allowed Grandpa to move them in. Space certainly wasn't a concern with five large bedrooms on the second floor. Since arriving on the edge of winter, there had not been much opportunity for exploring the outdoors, but Grae was itching to get out and explore the thousands of acres of pastures and rolling hills, the slaves' quarters, barns, Cedar Run Creek, the old iron forge, and even the cemetery, if spring ever decided to return.

They arrived just before Thanksgiving and since then she'd mainly tried to be invisible. As the only new student in the senior class, she became the center of attention and rumors. She arrived with a 4.0 grade point average in accelerated classes, so the teachers had grand expectations of her scholarly aptitude. Guidance counselors immediately began having long conversations with her about appropriate colleges. Grae knew her once padded scholarship fund was now non-existent and had most likely included other people's money. The counselors didn't seem to immediately know this tidbit of information and started naming Ivy League institutions. Grae just nodded, not wanting to leak her family history any sooner than necessary, but realized one day, when the word scholarship was mentioned, that the secret was out. If the counselors knew, then no doubt the students did.

Grae left her window seat and began walking through the house. Everything about their former home had been bright and new. It was a stark contrast to what she now saw and it affected her disposition.

"Hey, Miss Dreary Face, have you left your window perch to mingle with us common folks?" Grae had thought that it was fun having a little brother when she was younger, now she thought that being an only child might not be too bad.

"Peirce," Grae enjoyed calling Perry by his given name, it annoyed him. "Do you have to be breathing in my presence?"

"Watch it, Grae." Kat walked up behind her daughter. "That's not the kind of interaction I want to hear between you and your brother.

Grae sighed and ran up the staircase. She seemed to always get caught. "I'm going to my room. Call me when Perry has left for college." Her mother yelled something after her, but Grae chose to ignore it.

Standing at the doorway, she surveyed her room. She'd chosen this one in particular, not because of its blue walls, but for its two closets. Like just about every room in the house, it had a long history and according to some, she had a roommate.

In one corner was a full-length mirror that looked to be as old as the Mansion. Even in the old tainted glass, seeing her reflection, she saw the second reason why invisibility was impossible in her new world. Grae inherited most of her physical features from her mother. Her brilliant blue wide-set eyes seemed to simultaneously take on two different shades. As soon as she was old enough, she'd asked for contact lenses to mask this unusual feature, not for sight correction, but purely for aesthetics. Her long slender frame came from her father and made her a star on the basketball and volleyball teams. Yet she cast the illusion of being tall when she was only about five foot five. Grae had an agility that allowed her to stretch high and reach all the top shelves for her petite mother, but also gave her the ability to easily curve into that safe ball shape she so frequently preferred.

Her father's jet black hair crowned her head and she currently wore it straight with a part in the middle and a length that touched the midpoint of her back. It had a hint of blue to its sheen. Lately, she had noticed some whiteness developing near her forehead and had changed the angle of her part to hide it. One especially snotty girl at her former high school said the color could only come from an unnatural source, "Only dying your hair or being a witch could give you that color." Grae had wished for magical powers to make that girl disappear. She laughed softly now thinking that perhaps that girl had indeed disappeared. She ran her fingers through her hair, saying to herself, "It is a weird color."

"Not as weird as the girl who wears it."

Grae turned to find her brother leaning against the doorframe to her room; Perry was two years younger than her and already almost a foot taller. As dark as her hair was, his was almost that light. He had freckles across his nose and brown eyes like Grandpa Mack.

"Who asked you?"

Ever since they left Charlotte, their relationship had been strained. Perry liked it in Virginia and only saw it as a temporary move. He believed their father was innocent and that an appeal would soon result in his freedom. As close as he was to their mother, he refused to see how their Dad had treated her. Tom never laid a hand on his wife, but daily slapped her with words and belittling. Perry accepted his father's excuse that it was his way with their mother. Grae saw through the excuse, saw her mother's slumped shoulders, her nervous attention to make everything in the house perfect, her crying softly when she thought she was alone.

"You asked a question, I answered it. You don't see anyone else here do you?" Perry tumbled onto Grae's bed, shoes on her comforter.

"Feet off," she pointed. It was one of the few nice things she was able to bring from their home. In this dull, old room that hadn't been painted in her lifetime, it added a splash of color with its psychedelic pattern. "You're the one who says we have company here, that we are disturbing their space. Maybe I was talking to one of your dead friends."

Like their Grandma Belle, Perry sensed things that others did not. Grae didn't doubt that her brother had this ability; their mother had taught them to be open to things that were beyond their literal world. Grae just didn't care. Let the ghosts handle their own problems; she had enough of her own. It was fun to aggravate him about it, mainly because it was so unlike him otherwise. What good was communicating with the dead if you couldn't see the truth in the living? Their breathing mother had been belittled on almost a daily basis by the man who was supposed to love her. It seemed to Grae to be so contradictory, to only see parts of the truth.

"You know, Sis, if you weren't such a sarcastic pain in the rear, you might have more friends, living and dead." Perry jumped off the bed and walked out of the room. Before she could even turn back to the mirror, he returned. "Oh, Mom wants you to go to the store."

"Great!" Grae looked back into the mirror after Perry left. "Gav will probably be there, he usually works on Sunday afternoons. I don't want to see him."

There was no way that she could pawn this task off to Perry, who at 15, didn't have his license yet. Gav was another reason that she couldn't be invisible. Her jet black hair and olive skin gave her a strangely exotic look, something that had not escaped the eyes of the young men of the school. This immediately decreased her popularity with the girls, especially the popular ones. She didn't care about all the guys' attention, but those snobby girls didn't know that. She wasn't interested in their friendship anyway, but it made it hard to be friends with any of the girls; each little group seemed to have a different reason why they didn't want to associate with Grae White.

Except for one girl, her name was Carrie, and she was a junior. She didn't seem to be in anyone's group, yet no one was mean to her in any way that Grae could see. She had sought Grae out and thought she was cool. Grae was excited to make a friend until she found out why Carrie was so interested. "I can't believe that you live in the Mansion," Carrie said one day during lunch. "It's like my favorite place." Grae's look of confusion made Carrie explain. "It's SpookyWorld! I went to it five different times last fall. It was awesome!"

Every September, the owner and an army of volunteers transformed the Mansion and grounds into all the horror movies that ever invaded dreams. Thousands of people toured each weekend and saw a different side of the historic property. Kat brought her children up one October weekend several years earlier, and Grae was amazed at all the work that went into it. Since moving there, she hadn't thought about the fact that now she lived in SpookyWorld.

Grae didn't want a Spooky groupie and tried to avoid Carrie, but the girl seemed to be everywhere. Waiting at Grae's locker in the mornings, or saving her a seat in the cafeteria, and Carrie even changed her class schedule so they had the same study hall. It was hard not to be nice to her; she was so friendly and didn't ask her any personal questions. Carrie just seemed to accept Grae for who she was. But the girl was so bubbly, it really got on Grae's nerves, especially in the mornings. Then one day, as Carrie jabbered on about some scary something from the last spooky season, he sat down.

Grae was amazed that Carrie didn't stop talking. Most girls clammed up when a cute guy appeared within five feet. She'd seen this guy before, he was hard to miss. Body of a Calvin Klein underwear model, smile of a movie actor, and the hair of a rock star; everyone called him Gav, short for James McGavock. He was the quarterback of the football team, the captain of the basketball team, a star runner on the track team, and president of the senior class. Oh, and he was smart too…like Einstein smart. He was perfect, and, for some reason, he was sitting across from her opening a carton of milk, 2%, and there were three little cartons of it on his tray. Grae could feel about a hundred sets of female eyes on her, like ants crawling at a picnic; no matter how many were shooed away, more appeared to replace them. Every girl and many of the boys were watching, and all Carrie could do was talk about the chainsaw massacre guy in the barn.

"Carrot, is there anything else you can talk about? The whole room is trying to eat and doesn't want a description of a chainsaw man's decapitation skills," Gav said. He gave Grae a big Hollywood smile.

Grae watched as Carrie stopped talking, turned and rolled her eyes at Gav.

"Jockness, you just don't get it," Carrie said. "It's awesome, and Grae understands, she lives there." Grae longed to be invisible, literally, at that moment.

"You'll have to excuse my sister; she's really hung up on the horror stuff. I think she was adopted." Gav paused and flashed that smile again. "My name is James, but most people call me Gav. Please don't hold Carrothead against me."

"Sister? Carrie's your sister?" Grae looked back and forth at the two of them. They didn't look like siblings. Carrie had bright red hair, thus the Carrothead nickname. Gav's hair was lifeguard blond. Carrie had a face full of freckles; Gav had a dark tan, even in the winter. She would have never put them together in the same family.

"I'm afraid so," Carrie said. "It's really embarrassing since he is Mister Everything." Carrie paused and smirked at him. "You really didn't know that the Senior God was my brother, did you?"

Grae shook her head. She really hadn't thought about Gav at all. He seemed to be more the type of guy that you looked at, rather than thought about.

"That would be a first…a girl that hung out with me without wanting to get closer to this one."

Carrie's words struck Grae's heart. She could imagine that Carrie was befriended frequently by girls that only saw her as a way to get Gav's attention. They were hurtful, backstabbing girls, who once they got what they wanted or gave up, probably treated Carrie horribly. All Grae had seen was Carrie's SpookyWorld obsession. In reality, maybe all Carrie wanted was someone that might really be her friend.

TWO

"Grae! Come downstairs." Kat's voice brought Grae back to reality. Picking up a scrunchy, she pulled her hair back in a ponytail and grabbed her jacket from the bedpost. Maybe, she'd get lucky and Gav would be off today.

Grae found her mother in the Mansion's massive foyer at the bottom of the mahogany staircase. Even after living there for several months, Grae still had not gotten used to the size of each of the Mansion's rooms. It was a little overwhelming. Looking down from above, her mother's petite form looked almost doll-like. While Kat would now say that she was losing her looks, Grae thought her mother was beautiful. She was always amazed at how someone so small could command a room. She'd seen Kat spread her charm on PTA committees and school board meetings. She was a take-charge kind of woman, everywhere, but in her own married home.

"I need you to go to the store. Here's the list. There's a storm coming, as much as a foot of snow. I don't want us stuck without the basics."

"Snow? It was just raining earlier."

"That's weather in the mountains, Grae. Rain this morning, a blizzard tonight, by tomorrow the sun might melt it." Kat paused and noticed her reflection in the mirror hung in the foyer. She felt older than her 40s. She stopped dying her hair as it cost too much, and now her hair showed too much white. At least the stress lines across her forehead were easing. Maybe after another six months or so, Kat could start to relax. "This is not one of those times. The storm system looks pretty serious, I think you and Perry will get some snow days out of this one." Kat handed Grae the keys and some money. "There's a few extra dollars there, get us a couple of those five-day rental movies. Maybe something funny, no R-rated ones; something Grandpa might like watching with us."

Grae smiled as she walked out the door, her mother liked to add a little fun, even to a snow storm. As she walked around the Mansion to their vehicle, she looked out at the horizon. The sky had a strange ominous look. The heavy clouds were such a dark purple color that they were almost black. It was likely that a storm was imminent and it could be a serious one. From the corner of Grae's eye, she saw some movement near one of the buildings. She caught a glimpse of what appeared to be a small animal. Grae didn't have time to go chasing it, but figured it was the resident cat on the property. Grandpa had some strange name for it.

If they had still been in their old life, Grae would be driving her silver Mazda XS with the black leather-heated seats. It had an awesome stereo, and her father had purchased it right off the showroom floor with zero miles on it for her 16th birthday. It had become another casualty of their previous life and was impounded when her father was arrested. He'd become so sloppy at that point that he hadn't even tried to hide where the embezzled money was going. She really liked that car, but always felt like it didn't belong to her, and as it turned out, that feeling was right.

As she pulled into the parking lot of the small grocery store near the high school, she thought about how thankful her mother had been when the judge ruled that they would be allowed to keep one car, the oldest vehicle that they owned. It was a black Jeep Grand Cherokee with almost 75,000 miles on it, but at least it was theirs and would go in the snow. From the looks of the parking lot, the locals agreed that a storm was coming. There weren't many parking spaces to choose from and even fewer shopping carts when she went inside. Grae hoped that there was plenty of bread and milk still left and maybe some decent hamburger. On the list were many of the ingredients for chili and her mom's was the best. Kat had learned a lot about how to stretch a dollar in the last few months and making hearty soups and stews was one of her specialties.

After finding the first few items on the list, Grae stopped the cart in front of the meat department and surveyed what was left. The whole store looked as if the end of the world was coming. There were a few larger packages of ground chuck left. The list said to pick up three pounds. As she was putting a package into a plastic meat bag, someone hit her in the rear with a cart.

"Hey, watch it," she said, turning around. Her gaze followed the white butcher's apron to the name tag. "Gav," she said, as her eyes met his smile. "I didn't realize you would be here today." Grae wasn't a very convincing liar, so she hoped it didn't show.

"All hands on deck the day of a storm. There have been some crazy people in here today, but I didn't expect you to be one of them." There was that smile again. Grae wondered why he hadn't just gone to live in Hollywood; he could at least do toothpaste commercials.

"Well," Grae looked down at the list in her hand, "Mom needed me to come and get a few things. She's afraid it's going to snow, and we will get stuck in the boonies for days. I don't know since it was just raining this morning."

"You aren't used to winter in the mountains. We probably will get a ton of snow tonight. A few years ago, there was such a severe blizzard in March that they had to shut the interstates down."

"Really? I didn't know they could do that." That sounded kind of scary to Grae as she envisioned being stuck in the Mansion for a month. She might have to kill Perry and become the Mansion's newest mystery.

"Hey, um, I know this is a weird place for me to do this, but with the storm and all, I'm not sure when I will see you again. I was wondering…"

"Hi, Gav! Whatcha' doing?" Tatum Jones walked up and began talking. "Oh, wow, you look so cool in your white apron thing. Are you like the manager now or something?" Tatum was the cockiest of all the snobby senior girls, ruthless from what Grae had heard some say. Grae's Physics lab partner told her it was Tatum's goal to date all the jocks before she graduated. Gav was the only one left.

"Hey, Tatum." Gav seemed less than interested.

"My mom is like freaked over this storm. I don't think it will be any big deal." Tatum looked in Grae's direction. "Oh, hi, Grace, you shopping too?"

"Her name is Grae," Gav said, "and we were having a private conversation, if you don't mind."

It was obvious that Tatum wasn't used to guys talking to her that way. She looked back and forth at the two of them a couple of times, and then turned and stalked off.

"I don't think she liked that," Grae said. Gav actually looked a little mad. "It's okay if you want to go talk to her, I understand."

"Understand what? I haven't been able to stand her since we were seven years old. I'm tired of her chasing me so I can complete her senior tally." Gav's normally tan face was almost the color of the ground chuck Grae just placed in the cart. "I was about to ask you to the prom when she interrupted me."

Grae had never had a steady boyfriend like her friends in Charlotte did. She'd gone on a few dates, but she never really liked any of the guys enough to go out regularly. So it surprised her that after Gav said his last sentence that her heart got all fluttery and she felt her mouth get dry.

"Gav, come to the front please. Gav, come to the front." The loudspeaker interrupted that feeling and saved her from having to respond.

"Hey, I'll be back in a few minutes. You keep shopping, but don't leave without seeing me, okay?" When she didn't respond, he smiled. "Shake your head up and down." She shook her head, and he took off down the aisle closest to them.

Grae stood with her hands on the cart and stared in the direction that Gav had gone. She didn't realize that someone had come up behind her.

"Don't get any crazy fantasies. He's out of your league." She turned to see Tatum behind her. "I always get what I want and I want him. You're just the girl that lives in the haunted house. You're no one. Isn't your father in jail? Isn't he like a thief or something?" Tatum turned and started walking away.

"No, he's a murderer." Grae had no idea what she was saying. "You might want to be careful." Grae didn't turn to look; she just pushed the cart and went down the next aisle. "God, if mom finds out I said that, she will kill me," she mumbled to herself.

"Who are you talking to?" Gav was behind her again.

"Can't a girl have any privacy in this place?"

"Well, I just wanted to finish asking you that question." Gav paused and looked at the ground. Grae almost felt sorry for him. All of a sudden he looked very awkward.

"What was the question again?" Grae was afraid that she'd heard him wrong. She couldn't imagine that he wanted her to be his prom date.

Gav smiled, "You are just being a tease, aren't you? You know what the question was. You just want to make me ask again."

"Well, you didn't finish asking, and I wouldn't want to answer to the wrong thing." As if by magic all of the jitters that she felt just a few minutes earlier were gone, and she was so comfortable in his presence. Being with him, somehow, just felt familiar.

THREE

The snow came that night and all the next day. When it finally stopped, 20 inches covered the mountains that surrounded the Mansion with a thick blanket of bright, glistening white. It would be many days before Grae and Perry returned to school. Schools were rarely closed in suburban Charlotte and never for more than a day or two. Being out for a week was unimaginable. Excessively cold temperatures had accompanied the snow, which made driving extra hazardous. Rural back roads were slick, and snow drifts were abundant, making school bus travel not likely until the temperatures rose. The draftiness of the Mansion also meant they would be confined under many layers of clothing and near the house's many fireplaces.

"How in the world did anyone ever survive a winter in this old drafty place?" Perry said on their first morning of snow vacation as they had decided to call it.

"Well, that's why you see so many fireplaces throughout the house," Grandpa Mack said. "There needed to be a heat source in every room. It's also why they wore heavier clothes than we do now." He watched as his grandson played a handheld video game while sitting almost upside down on the sofa. "And they kept busy all the time, instead of sitting on their backsides wasting time with games. There were chores to be done."

Perry smirked. He was a gamer, no doubt about it, but that's what he and his friends had done in his previous life. "I miss Charlotte." Perry didn't mean to say that out loud. "I'm sorry, Grandpa. I like being here with you, but it's just not the same."

"It's all right, son, I understand. You've had a hard year. I know you miss your friends and your life there. I'm sorry you don't have it anymore." Grandpa Mack paused to gather his thoughts. "Sometimes the actions of others take a hold of our lives and all we can do is hang on." Saying that seemed to take a lot out of him, and he turned and left the room passing Grae as she entered.

"What just happened? Grandpa looks so sad." Despite his recent loss, Grandpa Mack usually didn't let his grief show.

"I'm not sure. We were just talking about how cold the house is, and I said I missed Charlotte, and then he just got sad." Perry sat up on the sofa. "It was really kind of strange. I didn't mean to upset him."

"Everything that happens in this house is strange." Grae sat in the floor several feet away from the fireplace. "Everything that brought us here is strange, too."

"Don't start in on Dad again." Perry walked to the window that faced the east. He touched the cold glass and the heat from his hand made an imprint. Grae watched as he removed his hand and the imprint began to fade away.

"I didn't say a word about Dad. It's just…well, everything seems weird. Living in this old place, there's even a blizzard outside. We haven't seen this much snow since we spent that Christmas skiing in Colorado."

Perry sat down next to Grae with his back to the fireplace. It made her shiver. "Is my position creeping you out?"

"You know how I feel about fire." Grae assumed her ball position with her back against an old chair. What had started as a simple story told to her as a child became a fear that bordered on obsessive. "I can't help it. Fire scares me, you know Dad's story."

"Yeah, but the fire was started by lightning, not from a fireplace." Perry rolled his eyes. "You've got to get over this. You've been a nervous wreck every time you've had to be near a fireplace here, and there is a fireplace in every room! Now you want to talk about something scary, that space heater in your room is scary."

Grandpa Mack had bought Grae a small space heater since there was no way she could have gotten any sleep with a fire lit. The story behind her fear was actually pretty simple. Their father grew up on a farm. One night there was a severe thunderstorm and lightning had struck a barn. The structure was quickly engulfed in flames, trapping the animals inside. Her grandfather and other members of the family awoke to see huge flames leaping from the barn through the windows of their two-story farmhouse. Somehow, they were able to get the animals out, but the fire could not be contained and completely destroyed the barn. It almost reached their home.

From that day on, every time a thunderstorm was looming, the family kept on alert, even in the middle of the night. It was a habit that followed Tom into his own family. Throughout her childhood, Grae would wake up during a stormy night and wander through the house. She would find her father sitting in the dark in a room with a window, watching and waiting for the storm to pass.

"Daddy, what are you doing?" Grae would ask.

It became a special time with her father, as she would climb into his lap and eventually fall asleep. "I'm keeping us safe," Tom

had said. "Keeping watch against what might try to hurt us."
Ironically, his actions would hurt most of all.

FOUR

With the knowledge that their snow vacation would confine them for several days, Grae and Perry decided that it was time to learn a little about their new home. Perry began exploring the upper floor above their bedrooms, but Grae decided that she was more interested in the people who had lived there. She knew there was a booklet of some sort that Granny Belle had created about the history of the house. She remembered her mother bringing one home after a visit. Granny Belle was helping the owner develop a tour of the house when she became ill. Grae thought if she could find one of those booklets, there was bound to be information about not only the Mansion, but those who had made it their home.

"Mom, do you remember that little book that Granny created about the Mansion?" Grae found Kat sitting in the kitchen with a cup of coffee and her laptop. From the look on her mother's face, she must have been working on her online banking. This task had created a line across her mother's forehead that Grae swore sometimes looked green as it undoubtedly had money worries attached to it.

"What?" Kat picked up the coffee cup and took a large drink.

"That little history book thing that Granny created a few years ago. You brought one home once; it had old photos in it and stuff about the house." Grae had never read the booklet because to her the Mansion was just a place where Grandpa worked. She never imagined she would do anything but visit it.

"Oh, yes, I remember that. She really worked hard on it. It was difficult to take a couple hundred years of history and create a tour that didn't last a whole day. I think I saw a box of them in the closet in the center of the house."

Grae left her mother and her worried look. She wondered how long it would take her to look happy again. It seemed that the past decade had all of a sudden caught up to her mother. Her once perfect appearance seemed more honest now. No more department store makeup and salon hair coloring to hide the stress of Kat's life. Her mother had been allowed to keep her once brimming jewelry collection, but she had sold several pieces so that there would be a small nest egg to start their new life. It had been strange to see her mother without all the outward layers that had been so familiar. It was like her mother had shed an artificial cocoon and now was a beautiful butterfly. As worried as her mother seemed at times, there was also a peace that engulfed her, a contentment in their new life.

The large closet in the foyer was a rare one in the Mansion. Built in a time before small storage areas had been the norm for homes, the Mansion had many rooms, but few storage areas. As Grae touched the doorknob, she heard a sound above her, sort of like a scamper.

"The strangeness is starting early today," she said to herself.

"It's probably a mouse." Perry had this irritating way of being nearby and not making his presence known until she was talking to herself. It was a double-edged tactic of his to not only scare her, but let her know that once again he'd caught her having a solitary conversation.

"One of these days, Perry, you are going to do that and I am going to do something drastic." While most teenage siblings exchanged banter using words like kill, murder, and maim to describe what they would do to each other, Grae and Perry were, at an early age, forbidden by their mother to ever say such things, even in jest. They'd never been told why, but after trying once and suffering the consequences, they learned not to take each other's lives in anger, even if only in the sibling humor sense.

"Ooooh, drastic. That's a new one. What will you do? Hide my shoes again? That just made Mom mad, didn't bother me at all."

"I wish I could go far, far away from you!" Grae sat down in the doorway of the closet and began opening a box. Being trapped inside this house with him was going to use up all her patience.

"Be careful what you wish for, Sis. You said it yourself, strange things happen here." Before she could reply, he disappeared into another room. Grae felt a shiver and rubbed her hands up and down her arms. She gazed up into the closet. She was pretty sure there wasn't a light bulb in the ceiling to illuminate her search, but someone had left a flashlight on the floor near the door hinges. She turned it on and began to look at the door beside her. Grandpa Mack had told them that all the doors in the house and the hardware on them were original. That would make the door over 125 years old. The iron in the hinges had even been made on the property. It was a hard concept for her teenage mind to grasp, but she couldn't help wonder about all the different people who had opened and closed that door during its life there. Maybe there were even secret hiding places in this house for other young women who needed to hide from their aggravating brothers.

She turned and faced into the closet, shining the light straight in front of her. At her eye level, she saw a spider staring back at her, dangling from a long web. Unlike most girls her age, spiders didn't really bother her, as long as they stayed in their space. She watched it as it quickly dropped to the floor and slid down a hole in the wood. As she tried to see where it was going, she touched a floorboard in the closet; a strange tilting feeling came upon her. For a split second, it was as if she was about to pass out. In her head, she heard a quick zapping noise like the sound a radio makes as it loses a station. She scooted herself until her back was leaning on the door and took several deep breaths.

"Maybe I need to have something to eat?" Grae said out loud as she rubbed her forehead. She sat there for a few more minutes, and then started looking in the closet again. There were several boxes on the floor in the front and the back. A couple of old umbrellas were leaning against the left side wall. One had an ornate handle and the faded fabric had a green calico design. Another was basic black with a very pointy tip and reminded her of the umbrella that Fred Astaire carried in *Singing in the Rain*. It was one of her mother's favorite films.

Up higher, she saw a row of hooks, and hanging on one was a black suede cowboy hat with a wide brim and a feather on the headband. Something about the hat made her smile. In the right hand corner was an old stick vacuum cleaner. Grae wondered if this had belonged to Granny Belle from when she had cleaned the Mansion for tours. The color red caught her attention in the far left corner. She would have to pull out the front boxes before she could tell what it was.

"What are you doing down there, little girl?" Grandpa Mack came up behind her; the sound of his heavy boots on the wood floor announced his arrival. From her vantage point on the floor, her grandfather looked different somehow. It was as if from this angle, she could see his past, the younger man he had once been. Black hair where grey was now, young smooth skin where beard stubble could be seen. For a moment, she saw a twinkle in his eye, a youthful optimism that now was replaced by the realities of old age and grief.

"Hey, Grandpa, I've been exploring the closet looking for Granny Belle's history brochure she made. Do you think it is in here?" At the mention of her grandmother's name, she saw the lines deepen around his eyes.

"You are in the right place. There's a box of Belle's little books in there and most of her research as well." He paused and looked over Grae at the contents of the closet. "It's hard to say what you may find in there. You never know what you will find in a room over nowhere."

"What? Over nowhere? Isn't the basement below this floor?"

Grandpa chuckled. "Yes, but right under the closet is a small stairway that goes right into the bottom of the closet. We call it the stairs to nowhere. No one knows why it is that way or where it may have once led. It's another one of this house's mysteries. Maybe someday we will know the truth." Grandpa Mack turned and headed toward the front door.

"Grandpa, is it okay if I go through this stuff?"

He turned and smiled. "It's just fine. Your grandmother would appreciate your interest. Maybe you and your mother could finish her research; I think that there was more to this project then that little booklet."

As Grandpa Mack walked away, Grae thought about the time she had spent a week one summer with her grandparents a couple of years earlier. Granny Belle was just starting to work on the research and would sit at the kitchen table with stacks of books, papers, and photographs around her. She tried to get Grae interested in the history of the Mansion, but Grae was more concerned about watching the Summer Olympics that week. She wished that she had spent more time learning about it.

The first box she pulled out contained what appeared to be those same documents Grae had watched her grandmother poring over. Many were photocopies of court records involving land transactions. Some were family genealogy documents including birth and death information. There were few photos, but the ones there seemed to indicate that no one smiled back then. Grae remembered learning something in school about how the process of photography was different in the beginning. People had to sit very still for several moments as the chemical process took effect. It was why portraits often had the subjects sitting in chairs with arm rests and could also explain why they didn't look too happy.

As Grae continued rummaging and reading, sitting in the floor in front of the closet, the stacks of papers and books grew around her. She was surprised to learn that the Mansion's history preceded the Civil War. The documents showed that the property's history went back almost one hundred years before that era.

After she realized that the documents covered such a wide range of time periods, Grae began making piles of the information by date. She took the piles into the dining room and placed them on a rarely used side table that would allow her space to keep the documents out of anyone's way.

As she reached the bottom of one large cardboard box, once used to house a large appliance, she noticed that a small envelope, almost the same shade of brown as the box, was lodged in one of the bottom flaps. She sat back down on the floor and turned the box on its side so that she could better reach it. She'd wedged herself toward the hinges of the door and was straddling the doorway. She just about had the envelope when Perry pushed the bottom of the box.

"Gonna set up residence inside there, Sis?"

"I might consider it if it would get me away from you." She finally got hold of the envelope, as her fingers grazed its edge; a strange feeling began to come over her, like she was falling backwards into a long hole. She lost her grip and found herself lying on the floor with Perry kneeling beside her.

"Grae, Grae, are you okay?" Perry shook her. She felt extremely hot and bitterly cold at the same time. "Grae, I'm going to go get Mom."

Before she could argue, he was running upstairs and yelling for their mother. Grae inched herself until she was sitting upright again. Her mother appeared in front of her and knelt beside her, feeling her forehead.

"Grae, honey, what happened? Perry says that you just collapsed in front of him. Did you faint?"

"Well, I…I don't really know. I just all of a sudden felt like I was falling backward."

"Have you ever felt this way before?" The worry lines were reappearing in her mother's forehead.

"Well, actually, a few hours ago, I sort of felt the same, only not as much. I've been here looking through these papers all morning, maybe something is messing with my allergies."

"What papers?" Her mother looked around. The only thing on the floor was the cardboard box.

"Oh, I forgot, I just took them into the dining room, to get them out of the way. They're Granny Belle's research documents. Grandpa said it was okay if I looked through them."

"I'm sure it is fine, dear. But right now I'm concerned about you. Do you feel sick on your stomach?" Kat felt her daughter's forehead again and the back of her neck. "You really don't seem to have a fever, but you are kind of clammy."

"No, I don't feel sick, just strange." Grae sat completely up and started to stand.

"I think you should sit here another few minutes. Perry, go and get Grae something to drink, maybe a Coke if we have some." Kat returned her gaze to Grae. "When Perry gets back, we are going to help you into the living room and you are going to rest a while. I'm going to fix us all some lunch. It's probably just your allergies or maybe a little low blood sugar, but I want you to let me know if this happens again."

Grae took the scrunchy out of her hair and ran her fingers through it. She didn't want her mother to be worried about her. "Okay."

"Graham Belle White, you will tell me if you experience this again. It could be serious." Kat began to rub her own forehead.

"I will, Mom." Grae took hold of her mother's hand, just as she had done every day as a small child. The gesture brought a smile to her mother's face. A tear escaped her eye. "I don't want you to worry about me," Grae said. "You have too much to worry about as it is. I will be fine."

"Worrying about you and your brother is my job." Kat paused. "I love you both deeply; you are all I have that is truly mine."

FIVE

Grae spent the rest of the afternoon on the couch. Even though she promised to rest, her mother wouldn't let her read any of the documents that she had found that morning. Fearful that Grae might have experienced an allergic reaction to dust, mold, or the general oldness of the papers, she wanted Grae to have at least 24 hours for her lungs to recover. Since television reception was almost non-existent on the hilltop, Grae decided to begin reading one of the books that was assigned for an upcoming book report. The book was *The Grapes of Wrath*.

A few years earlier, Grae's mother had undergone gall bladder surgery and was forced to rest for several days. Her father had allowed Grae to stay out of school and help her mother. Grae wouldn't let Kat lift anything heavier than the remote and they had watched three days' worth of old movies. Kat had a special fondness for Jimmy Stewart, but had insisted that they watch this Hollywood classic version of the novel, a Henry Fonda film, for educational purposes.

"Every senior has to read *The Grapes of Wrath*," Kat said. "You might as well have a preview." While Grae at first found the movie extremely dreary, as most black and white movies were to her generation, after a while the story started to grow on her and she began to wonder what life was really like during the Depression.

As she began reading the first chapter, her mind began to wander back to the Mansion and all the history that was trapped in the memory of the walls around her. She'd seen some of the layers of paint and wallpaper throughout the house and wondered about all the different lives that each layer represented. What little she knew about the families who lived there seemed steeped in mystery and tragedy. Like the novel she was reading, the history of the house and those who had passed through it had been filled with many highs and lows. But somehow, like the Joad family travelling west, the Mansion had lived on and carried a legacy in its very existence.

Shortly after dinner, Grae told her mother that she was going to take a shower and go to bed early. "I'm fine. Don't get that look. All this resting has worn me out." Kat rolled her eyes.

"That sounds more like you," Kat laughed. "I will check on you before I go to bed. Hope there is plenty of hot water. I did a load of towels an hour ago."

Grae climbed the staircase. There was only one shower in the house. It was downstairs near the center of the house. Grandpa and his crew were in the process of adding another bathroom upstairs, but it would be a while before it was finished. Kat's mother had gotten each of them a small tote to put all their toiletries in so that they could easily carry them down and not clutter the already small space. It was another one of the drastic changes they had experienced. Their large home in Charlotte had six bathrooms. Grae never had to share her sink, toilet, garden tub or walk-in shower with anyone. Even when she invited a friend over, there was a bathroom available for her guest. Kat had joked then that Grae would never survive living in a dorm and sharing a bathroom with a dozen other girls. She was now having a trial run of that experience with her own family.

Grae went to the closet in the far right corner of the room and found that all the contents of the tote were on the closet floor. It wasn't like it had fallen over or been dumped out, each item was placed in a row beside it. It was a perfectly straight line of little bottles and containers. At first it made her smile, it was so orderly. Then it started ticking her off. Only one person could have done this.

"Perry!" Grae yelled at the top of her lungs. "Perry White! You get your infuriating self up here right now!"

Hearing her daughter's voice, Kat was the first one up the stairs. "What's wrong Grae? Are you okay?" Kat found Grae standing in front of her closet, hands on her hips, tapping her foot. Kat knew that stance, someone had made her mad.

"PERRY! I mean it, if you don't get up here right now; I'm going to make you wish you were never born!"

"Graham White! You watch your mouth, young lady. You know that you are not to threaten your brother."

"But, Mom, look what he did!" Grae pointed to the items on the floor.

"What? He straightened up your stuff? I don't see what you are so riled up about."

"No, he took all my stuff out of my tote, just to get under my skin."

Perry walked into the room. "What's going on? Why are you yelling?"

Grae walked around her mother. When she reached Perry, she started poking her finger in his chest. His growth spurt the previous summer had created a significant difference in their height. "You keep messing with my stuff and I'm gonna…"

"Grae, stop it!" A scream from their mother rendered silence to both Grae and Perry. "Perry, why have you been in your sister's room?"

"What are you all talking about? I've not been in here without Grae the whole time we've lived here."

"Then how do you explain that?" Grae turned to point to the closet, but all of the toiletries items were now back in the tote. Grae gasped and so did her mother.

"What is wrong with the two of you? You look as if you've just seen a ghost."

Kat's mother took a hold of Grae and Perry's arms and led them out of the room. "I think it's time we had a family talk."

The three of them walked into the living room where Grandpa Mack was sitting in an old leather recliner. He'd brought it from his home, one of the few personal pieces of furniture he had not put in storage. "It fits my butt," he'd told Kat when she had seen it sitting in the center of the living room when they moved in. "It's taken me 25 years to get it broken in. It probably has more years left in it than I do." Kat knew that it had been a long standing bone of contention between her parents and that her mother had banished Old Brown, as she called it, to the den years earlier.

"Are we in trouble?" Grandpa said with a grin. "I heard some yelling."

"Well, Dad, I think it's time that we told these two about Clara's room and some other things."

"Oh," Grandpa Mack put the recliner in its upright position. "Well, that's not a short story, is it?"

"Your stories never are." Kat smiled.

Grandpa Mack took off his John Deere cap and ran his fingers through his full head of salt and pepper hair. He set the cap down on the end table next to his chair. It was also a relic of his past, the kind of table that is also a lamp and a magazine holder. He kept his *Farmer's Almanacs*, his *Grit* magazines, and the daily issue of the *Roanoke Times* in the side pockets.

"Well, kids, this house has a history. You don't live as long as it has and not have a few skeletons in the closets."

"Oh, Dad, quit kidding around. Clara's made herself known in Grae's room."

Grae and Perry looked at each other and back at their mother. "Clara? Who is Clara?" Grae was feeling faint again. "This has been too weird of a day."

"You know, Kat, this could be why she isn't feeling well."

"I know, Dad, but let's not get ahead of ourselves."

"Someone please tell us what you are talking about!" Perry was starting to pace the floor. It was his way of dealing with stress.

"Okay, both of you sit down." Kat motioned to her children to sit on the sofa next to the window.

"Kids, you know, I've spent a lot of time in this house throughout my life." Grandpa Mack stood up and walked toward the fireplace. "Our family's history and this house's original family have been intertwined for hundreds of years. As a child, I played here. As a young man, I worked here. For some reason, everything I have done in my life has led me back here. And now, you all are here with me."

Grae and Perry had always enjoyed their grandfather's stories. But, from the tone of his voice, it didn't seem that this story would be as amusing as the rest.

"This house is home to me in many ways, a heritage home, I guess," Grandpa continued. "This is the first time that I have ever lived here, but I know more about it than most. It was one of the things your grandmother enjoyed most, hearing my stories. She even wrote some of them down." He leaned his arm on the mantle of the fireplace and absentmindedly moved a small old picture frame. "But the stories aren't all happy ones. There's been a lot of sadness in this house, a lot of tragedy, and sometimes sadness stays behind long after the incident is over."

Grae and Perry leaned back on the sofa. They both seemed to simultaneously realize that Grandpa's talk was going to take a while. It was almost ten o'clock and Grae and Perry's eyes were growing heavy as Grandpa Mack began to talk about Clara.

"There's not a lot known about Clara. It seems that everything about her and her little life proved to be a secret. But the story goes that her parents died and that Bettie and Emily Graham took her in and hid her in that room. They were the daughters of Squire David Graham, and it appears that he was quite the ruler of the house in his day. He locked up his wife, Martha, and wouldn't let her have any contact with her children. His reasons were a mystery, but he was very much the authoritarian. His children must have had some defiance in them though, especially Bettie, to have hidden a child in the house."

"I don't understand, Grandpa," Perry said. "What was the connection between Clara and the Graham family? Was she a neighbor?"

"Don't know for sure, but there's one story that says her father delivered milk here. I guess I've just wondered if he didn't get to know the family through delivering and then maybe he and his wife became ill. Who knows? He might have left little Clara here hoping the family would take her in."

"But that still doesn't explain why you think she was in my room? Did she grow up and move away and live to be an old lady?" The entire day was catching up with Grae, exhaustion was setting in, and nothing seemed to be making sense anymore.

Grandpa Mack looked at Kat. "Go ahead, Dad, they've got to hear it all."

"Well, Grae, this story doesn't have a happy ending. If you keep reading your grandmother's papers you are going to find that most stories in this house do not. It's thought that Clara was about seven or eight; we're not sure how long she lived here. She might have come here sick." Grandpa shook his head and released a deep sigh. "But back then, they didn't have much medicine. She had influenza or pneumonia, or maybe both. Sometime thereafter, she died."

"In Grae's room?" Perry said, eyes bulging with shock.

"Yes, we assume so."

"Well, people die, happens all the time." Grae said flippantly, trying not to let the chill that had just crossed her body show. "It doesn't mean that she's a ghost or anything."

Kat sat down on the sofa between her two children. "There's more to the story."

"If you can't tell your father that you have an orphaned child staying in your room, you sure can't tell him when she dies." Grandpa Mack walked toward the window. "Squire David must have been a real son of a…"

"Dad, watch the language."

"Ah, Kat, these kids have heard worse. The truth doesn't hurt anybody." He turned and looked out at the now glistening blanket of snow that was refreezing as the temperature continued to drop. "They had to hide her body. Story goes that they wrapped her up in sheets and kept her in the closet. Not sure how long that went on. It was winter time and when they did manage to sneak her out, they really couldn't dig a grave, the ground was too hard. So, they basically just stacked stones on top of her."

Grae's olive skin had gone pale and she had that cold clammy feeling again. "They hid her body in the closet where I keep my bathroom tote."

"Yes," Kat said, putting her arm around her daughter. "But there is no reason to be afraid."

Grae stood up and looked back at her mother. "Oh, no, no reason at all. I'm just living with some dead girl in my room that likes to put things in a row." Grae began pacing. "Sorry, Perry, but that's the best excuse ever for you not doing something. Let's blame the dead girl."

"Graham Belle, now that's enough. You need to be respectful." Kat stood up and took hold of her daughter's shoulders, facing her. "I've always taught you and your brother to be open minded to the possibility of things beyond our physical world."

"Yeah, yeah, but you never said we would have to share a room with one! Carrie is right. I do live in SpookyWorld!"

"Grae, stop it! I know this is unnerving, but you've got to calm down and think about it."

Grae shook her head and wrenched herself from her mother's grasp. "I'm sure that's all I'm going to be doing is thinking about it."

"Honey, you can switch rooms if you want," Grandpa said. "There are plenty of other rooms for you to sleep in."

"Right, who died in them? Maybe even a murder or two. Can you say for a certainty which room someone didn't pass away in? And what does that mean anyway? They didn't leave!"

"Well, there are a few other rooms that we know someone died in, but I'm sure that we can find one…"

"Maybe the kitchen? Did anyone die there?" Perry had decided to chime in.

"Really funny, bro, wait till you hear the story about your room."

"Enough!" Kat clapped her hands. "Everyone sit down." Grae and Perry grumbled as they went back to the sofa. "I said everyone." Kat eyed her father who used the opportunity to try to break the tension by making a face. No one laughed. He sat down. "Yes, it is a little disturbing to know that someone died in your room. But remember something; it is not unusual for someone to die in a home. It happened very frequently at that time because there were not as many hospitals or doctors in an area. But it's not that rare, even today."

Kat calmed her voice before she continued. "She was just a little girl and she spent the end of her natural life in a strange place. Her parents were gone. She was probably very scared and then she became sick and died. There's nothing happy about her story. But I used to play with her when I was little, and I swear sometimes I think I heard her laugh." Kat smiled and shook her head.

"You played with her?" Perry looked at his mother with a confused expression.

"When I was a child, we would come here occasionally and Dad would do some repairs on the house. The owner then was a real character, eccentric."

"Strange, just say it, Katie, he was strange." Grandpa Mack laughed and leaned back in the recliner. "But I liked him. He was a straight shooter, and he always paid me in cash, hundred dollar bills, crisp, liked he'd just made 'em."

Perry smiled big at that description. "Sure wish he was still around. I'd like to find some people like that to mow for this summer."

"We can work on that." Grandpa thought for a moment. "Oh, I bet there would be several people in the neighborhoods around here."

"Can we please get back to Clara?" Grae rolled her eyes and adjusted her arms around her legs, she was in her ball position. "I still don't understand what you are trying to tell me, Mom. You act like having Clara around is a fun thing."

"Well, honey, I don't mean that it is not a little unnerving. Seeing things move around your room and such. Maybe hearing noises in the night. But I can assure you that if it is Clara, she's more afraid of you."

Kat sat down in the floor in front of her daughter. "We've talked about this before. I don't know how to explain what happens to a person when they die. Does their spirit continue? Do they go somewhere else? Do they become energy and linger? Do the circumstances of their death influence what happens? There are medical theories and religious theories and just plain theories. I'm not sure what I believe, and maybe it's a combination of all of that or none of it. But I do know this, every life that passes through this world leaves a little of itself behind. If we encounter someone else's life, living or dead, we should be respectful. If a part of Clara is here with us, we should treat her kindly. She has just as much right to be here as we do."

Grae relaxed her position and put her feet back on the floor. "Well, I guess I can give her some space. It's weird to think about someone I can't see moving my stuff around."

"I know, but really, who knows what is in this world around us that we can't see? We accept those scientific things we learn about. Information is flying through the air all around as we use those electronic devices that you are so attached to. Well, science can't explain Clara, and why she may be here. But it doesn't mean that it isn't possible. You know one thing that your father and I always agreed on, you both heard us say this, there is so much that we don't know. There's a vast universe of knowledge, humans have only really tipped the iceberg. We've got to keep our minds open to possibilities. We've got to be seekers of truth, whether we like what we learn or not."

"Okay, Mom," Grae said. She gave Perry a nudge.

"Yeah, yeah. But I want to know who died in my room?" Kat threw a pillow at her son as Grae got up and walked out of the room.

"Where are you going?" Kat asked.

"To my room to gather up my stuff, I still want to take a shower."

"It's kind of late, but I guess it might make you feel better. You want me to come with you?"

"No, I think I need to do this on my own." As Grae walked up the stairs, she thought about what her mother had just said. "Seekers of truth, I like that."

"Hey, Mom," Grae said as she climbed the staircase. "I think that if we all ate s'mores we would feel better."

"Well, I think I could arrange that."

Grae started to yell a reply as she walked through the doorway of her room, but the shock of what she saw stifled any further comment. She wasn't sure that her feet actually touched the steps as she flew down the staircase. It was almost as if she had literally grown wings, because all she felt was a breeze where her feet should have connected with the wood. She was surprised that she hadn't screamed, but her vocal chords didn't seem to be working. Arriving back in the living room, she found that her family had already scattered and only her grandfather remained.

"That was quick, Buttercup." Seeing that her mouth was open and nothing was coming out, Grandpa quickly stood up. "Are you okay?" All Grae could do was point. "Kat, get in here. Something's happened."

Kat ran from the back of the house and found them both standing in the foyer. "What's wrong?" Once again, nothing would come out of Grae's mouth, so she took hold of her mother's hand and pulled her as they ran up the steps. As they entered her room, Grae pointed to her bed.

When a house is packed up in a fairly quick manner, sometimes items don't get divided into boxes as they should. When an angry teenager, who doesn't want to move, packs up her stuff, it's just a mess. That's why Grae's childhood Barbie dolls were in the same box with her shoes. She'd recently opened that particular box to find her winter boots.

When Kat looked at the psychedelic bedspread, lying next to Grae's calculus book she saw two Ken dolls dressed only in shorts with yarn around their necks like nooses. Kat gasped.

Grandpa just shook his head. "Well, I guess Clara has met Bob and Sam," he said.

It was more than Grae could grasp. All the names she had never heard, all the things out of place. She'd been standing in the doorway, but as Grandpa made his last statement, her feet slowly started leaving the floor and her body began to fall. The room spun, she smelled a foreboding odor like the strong vinegar Granny Belle used for her dill pickles mixed with the scent of an old cigar, and it began to make her sick. Her vision blurred, and then there was darkness.

SIX

When Grae awakened, everything was so bright in front of her, she was afraid she had died and was seeing the light that was so prevalent in near-death stories. As her vision slowly came into focus, she realized that she was in a hospital. She reached for the metal railing and felt the tug of an IV on her hand. Looking around, she saw that several machines were around her bed like the ones she had seen Granny Belle hooked to before she passed. The sight scared her and made her say the name of the one person who could give her comfort.

"Mom," Grae's voice was barely above a whisper, but her mother's ears instantly heard it from the doorway where she was standing with a nurse.

"Yes, Grae, I'm here. How are you feeling, baby?" Kat's eyes were swollen and her mascara was little puddles in the corners of her eyes.

"I don't know." Grae looked around, everything was still fuzzy. "Everything looks blurry."

"That's okay, Grae," a young nurse said as she took Grae's hand and checked the IV. "We've given you a little medicine to make you sleepy. Does anything hurt? How about your head?"

"I, I don't think so. My throat feels strange."

"Grae, do you remember anything that happened to you earlier?"

"I remember we were all in my room and Grandpa was talking, and then everything went black."

"You rest, dear, and I'm going to go out to the waiting room and send Grandpa in."

Kat and the nurse walked out into the hallway. "Missus White, has Grae ever had an episode like this before?"

"No, never." Kat folded her arms in front of her.

"The blood work didn't indicate anything to cause this, but there could be some residual effects. Could Grae be using any drugs?"

"Oh no, not Grae, she's really a good kid. She's really kept to herself mostly since we've moved here."

"Any history of psychosis in the family, even in past generations?"

"No." Kat really didn't like this line of questions.

"Can you think of anything that might explain why she experienced this psychotic episode? Anything she was exposed to recently? Trauma of any sort?"

Kat watched as the nurse waited pen in hand, for her to respond. She couldn't exactly tell the nurse that her daughter's room had been rearranged by a ghost, could she? She couldn't lie, so she did the next best thing. She told the truth.

"My husband was just put in prison. Does that count?"

The nurse's eyes got big. "Well, I would say that would qualify as traumatic. What did he do?"

"He stole 15 million dollars." Kat didn't wait for her to react. She turned and headed toward the waiting room to find the rest of her family. She would take Grae home and they would deal with this as a family.

Grae slept on the way home, the effects of the sedation still apparent. Grandpa Mack carried her into the Mansion, and Kat created a little sleeping nest for her on the couch in the living room with many blankets and pillows.

"What happened to me?" Grae drowsily looked around the room.

"We're not exactly sure," Grandpa said. "You blacked out and fell to the floor upstairs. We tried for several minutes to get you to wake up. It wasn't working so we put you in the Jeep and slid out of here."

"Slid?" Grae began to drink the big mug of tea that Grandpa handed her. Grae breathed in the familiar aroma. Her mother knew what would make her feel better. It was chai tea, her favorite, with extra sprinkles of cinnamon and a little milk. Cinnamon toast also stood waiting, but Grae's stomach was not quite ready to accept it. Cinnamon had a calming effect on Grae, it was comforting.

"It was very cold out there last night and the roads hadn't been treated," Grandpa Mack said. "But nothing was gonna keep this old man from getting his Grae Belle to the hospital." Grandpa patted Grae on the head. "You woke up after we reached the hospital, but you weren't yourself. You kept fighting the nurses and screaming. The look in your eyes was as if you weren't there with us."

Grae looked over at her brother. He was lying upside down on a chair, sound asleep. It was a familiar position for him. She remembered him in his baby bed sleeping with his feet up on the rails. Grandpa sat down in his chair and began to drink coffee and read the newspaper.

"Grandpa, I don't remember any of that. What happened to me?"

He set his coffee cup down and folded his newspaper. "Sweetheart, I really don't know. You seemed to have left us for a while." Grandpa rubbed his forehead. "Your mother doesn't want us to talk about it, but I think you need to know. It was almost as if your eyes were seeing something that your mind couldn't process, so it shut off. The words you were saying made no sense."

"What did I say?" Grae pulled the blankets around her and sank further down into the pillows.

"You kept saying 'untie me' and you were pulling your arms like they were tied behind your back. You were moving around so much that the nurses wanted to restrain you, but your mother wouldn't allow it. So she got in the bed with you and held you down." Grandpa stopped talking and sat on the edge of the couch next to Grae. "I know you are scared, but I really think your mind just had too much to grasp today. You were tired and stressed and shocked all at the same time and your mind said 'Enough!'" Grandpa paused and watched Grae for a few moments. "Get some rest and get up tomorrow and do whatever you want. But don't be afraid of this house, it's your home now. It's just brick and wood and whole lot of memories, but it's not going to hurt you."

"But, Grandpa, what about what Clara did? Shouldn't that scare me?"

"I really don't think so. Clara has been here for a very long time. I can't explain it or understand it. I stopped trying years ago. Some don't believe it at all. But, when you see with your own eyes that things have moved without a living soul's touch or hear something soft and gentle like the whisper of a little girl's voice, you can't help but believe that there is a little lost one nearby. Don't let it scare you, it's not her fault, she's just trying to make a connection."

"Those dolls, Grandpa! They had strings around their necks. That's a strange way to play with them."

"I've been thinking about that. I think she was trying to tell us something." Grandpa went back to his old brown chair. "That part is rather confusing; because I think what she is trying to tell us about happened long before she was alive, before this house was even here."

"Okay, that's enough of this discussion for now. Grae needs to sleep," Kat said, as she appeared in the doorway. "Dad, you should get some rest too."

"Someone really needs to wake up Perry," Grae said. "He's been in the same position for over an hour. He looks like a bat. We certainly don't need a vampire around here with everything else."

Kat laughed at her son, still sleeping upside down. "I should have put him in gymnastics class when he was little. He can certainly maneuver his body into a lot of different shapes."

"Yeah, well, he would have looked great in those pink tights," Grae laughed as she rolled over on the couch.

"I heard that." Perry grunted.

Kat shook her head and smiled.

Grae slept the majority of the afternoon and amazingly continued through the rest of the night. By morning, she was two things, sore from lying around and incredibly hungry.

"Mom, I think I need one of your super breakfasts," Grae finally had the shower she wanted two days earlier. Everything in her room seemed in place. All her items were inside her bathroom tote and the Ken dolls were gone from her view. It was almost as if the recent incident had not occurred. She knew that she could pretend that, but she had to grasp what had happened and figure it out. For now, she could push that reality away long enough to eat one of her mother's famous breakfasts. She was starving.

"Well, that's great to hear! I was hoping you might feel that way and have already gotten started." Kat's time as a housewife hadn't encouraged her career in finance, but it had paved the way for one skill that her family dearly loved, she had become an incredible cook. She could read any recipe and master it. She could watch any cooking show and immediately go to the kitchen and make the dish. Tom had encouraged this talent and because of it, Kat had a kitchen that would make a commercial chef envious. While the large appliances stayed with the house, her small appliances and tools came with her as well as her kitchen tablet, as she called it; a small laptop with an incredible collection of cookbooks and meal planning software.

Sunday mornings at the White's house were deemed sacred. No matter what anyone in the family was doing, at 10 o'clock everyone made their way to the kitchen to see what Kat's breakfast masterpiece would be. It might have included aromatic eggs benedict, creamy quiche Lorraine, a stack of French toast with whipped cream and fresh fruits, or an assortment of muffins and pastries. Sometimes the menu would be far simpler but Kat would always give it her own unique flair. She could make the most unusual biscuits and gravy, and omelets that were out of this world.

In anticipation of her daughter feeling better, Kat had begun around dawn preparing the ingredients to Grae's favorite breakfast. The menu would include French toast dipped in slivers of almonds and coconut with peaches and whipped cream. It would be served with cheesy scrambled eggs that included Parmesan and Swiss cheeses as well as whipping cream. Grae might feel differently when she was in her twenties and carefully counting all her calories, but for someone who had not really eaten in two days it would hopefully come as a welcomed meal.

As Grae sat with her family in the old dining room, she thought about all that had happened since the winter storm forced them on a snow vacation. She knew it would be easy to ignore these developments and go back to her regular teenage life as the snow melted over the next few days. But, even more clearly, she knew that she must discover what was really going on in this house. She must discover the truth behind the legends and stories.

After the super breakfast, Grandpa Mack took Perry to survey the condition of the roads on the property and the main road below the house. Kat tackled kitchen clean-up and more cooking; making breakfast had put her in a creative cooking mood.

Grae took this opportunity to return to the stacks of documents she had gone through two days earlier. The stacks were right where she left them, on the side table in the dining room. It was nice when things stayed in place.

Since Grae was alone, she decided to do her reading in her preferred manner, aloud. It was a habit started when she was just learning how to read. She'd had a little difficulty with speech at that age and reading out loud in class terrified her. Her mother arranged for a neighbor, a nice lady named Miss Megginson, to tutor her three afternoons a week for several months. She was a speech pathologist and her easy, patient manner had worked miracles with Grae. It wasn't long before she was winning oral essay contests and trying out for roles in middle school and high school theatrical productions. Miss Megginson had taught her that there were two reasons to read aloud whenever you had the opportunity. One was that it was good practice of your oratory skills, and the other was that you would better retain the information you were reading. You saw it, you said it, and you heard it.

So Grae began to read aloud from her grandmother's history booklet. "The property on which the Major Graham Mansion now stands was known in its early days as Cedar Run Farm. Squire David Graham bought 2,000 acres, log cabins, out buildings, barns, and an iron-making furnace from the Crockett family for $10,000 in 1826. Previously, 187 of those acres and some of the log cabins along Cedar Run Creek were home to

Joseph Joel Baker and his family and slaves. He was murdered by his slaves 'Bob' and 'Sam' in May of 1786." Grae felt the hairs on the back of her neck stand up. "Bob and Sam, those were the names that Grandpa used. He said that Clara must have met Bob and Sam. Oh no, I wonder if this document will tell me how they died?"

"Hey, Sis, who are you talking to now?" Perry suddenly was behind her.

"If I am ever found dead of shock, I hope someone asks you if you scared me to death." Grae rolled her eyes.

"Yeah, well, just don't haunt me or something." Perry laughed. I'm sorry; I really didn't mean to scare you. I was just wondering if someone was really here." Perry sat down at the table next to Grae. "So what are you reading? I heard a little bit as I was coming down the hall. Something about Bob and Sam?"

"I've been reading about the history of the house." Grae read to Perry what she had learned so far.

"Weren't those the names Grandpa used when we found those Ken dolls in your room?"

"Yes, and I have a feeling that if I read further I am going to find out that they were hung for their crime." Grae began to shuffle through a few more papers. "It's true. This one says that the local sheriff arrested Bob and Sam; they were put on trial, and then hung, possibly on this property. The sheriff was paid 200 pounds of tobacco for his trouble."

"That's a lot of cigarettes," Perry said with a chuckle.

"I remember learning in history class that growing tobacco was a really serious industry during the first hundred years or so of America. It was really valuable, and I think it was like the only thing that America exported in the beginning. It was used like money."

"Two hundred pounds of tobacco is still a lot of cigarettes," Perry said.

Grae shook her head. "There's lots of information in these documents of Granny's about the Graham family, but I don't see much about the Bakers except the murder."

"Did his family move away after he died?"

"I guess some of them might have, but his son, John, was the one that sold some of this land to Squire Graham."

"Squire? That sounds weird. Did it mean something like Mister?"

"I don't know, if you really want to be helpful, why don't you Google it and find out?"

"Okay, but I don't promise to be right back because you have just given me permission to be on the computer and you know what that means?"

"An all-night gaming session, I bet! You better not let Mom catch you."

"I'll just tell her that you told me I could."

"Get out of here, Perry."

"That would be Squire White to you."

Grae spent the rest of the afternoon reading the yellowing pages. As it started getting dark, she discovered a page that appeared to be from a genealogy book. It was the family tree for Joseph Baker.

"You've been in here all afternoon, Grae," Kat said as she came in and turned on the overhead light. "Aren't your eyes getting tired?"

"A little bit, Mom, but it's actually getting a little interesting. Do you know about the Baker family that used to live on this property?"

"Hmm, a little bit. I don't think they were here very long. Something tragic happened."

Grae could tell that her mother was trying to avoid discussing what had happened. "Yes, I would call a murder, and then hangings tragic."

"Oh, you know about that. I guess it would be in your grandmother's history papers."

"I want to understand what happened, and why those two slaves killed Mister Baker."

"I think the legend says that Mister Baker had promised them their freedom upon his death, perhaps they just wanted to speed that along." Kat sat down next to Grae and began looking through some of the papers.

"I suppose that could be true. I've read that in several places, but something just doesn't make sense to me. Joseph Baker was in his thirties when he died, so why was he promising something to his slaves that if he had died of old age, wouldn't have happened for quite a while?"

Kat smiled at her daughter. "You have always liked to figure things out, and you often see a side not as visible to the rest of us. But, you know, old age wasn't as old as it is now. There were a lot of diseases that took people much younger then."

"I know, but Joseph Baker didn't know when he was going to die. It just doesn't seem quite right."

"Well, I guess that's something that will have to remain a mystery. I doubt that there are any other accounts that you can find." Kat walked over to the window.

"Too bad I didn't take that class in time travel while we were still in Charlotte." Grae waited for a response. Her mother remained silent. "Are you okay? I made a really sarcastic comment, and you didn't respond. Did you hear me?"

A tear ran down Kat's face on the side opposite from where Grae was standing. "I heard you, Grae. Just don't joke about that."

"Time travel? But why? It's not real or anything."

"Just because you haven't done it, doesn't mean it isn't real. What do you think Clara was doing?"

"Well, that's like, well, she's dead. Time doesn't mean anything if you're dead."

"Says who?"

"I don't know, I guess I never thought about it."

"Grae, only believe something is impossible if you know it isn't possible."

"That sounds like a riddle, Mom."

"And everything in this universe is."

SEVEN

The snow was starting to melt, but not quite enough to make the rural roads safe for a school bus. No school bus, so no school, which was just another weird part of Grae and Perry's new home. The previous days had made them feel like they were stranded on another universe. They had never been "cooped up," as Grandpa Mack said, for so long. It was one of the many adjustments their new life was forcing them into.

One of the hardest had been not having a cell phone. They had both been very attached to their phones in Charlotte. Always having the latest version since they were in elementary school, it was sort of like having shoes or a backpack, you just did. But the move meant lots of sacrifices, and Kat couldn't afford for her children to have phones right now. Everyone at their new school had one, it seemed, but not them. When spring came, hopefully there would be part-time jobs for them and the money for this piece of technology.

There were very few phone calls for any of them since they'd moved into the Mansion. No one they knew seemed to understand how a land line worked any more. It was surprising that morning when the phone in the foyer rang.

"Hello," Grandpa Mack said. "Yes, she lives here…What's your name?...Well, yes, I guess so….Grae! Telephone!" Grandpa laid the phone down as Grae came running down the stairs. "He says his name is James McGavock. Now there's a name that's not a stranger to this house."

Grae had a puzzled look on her face as she picked up the phone, "Hello."

"Hey, Grae, this is Gav."

"Hi, Gav." Thankfully, the phone was at least cordless and she could pace down the long foyer.

"How have you been doing? It was some kind of storm, huh?"

"Oh, I've been fine." She wasn't about to mention her trip to the hospital and what lead to it. "It was a lot of snow. I've never been out of school this long for the weather."

"Yeah, I guess that doesn't happen so much in the city. It will probably be a few more days before we get back to school. What have you been doing with yourself? Hope you haven't been aggravating your brother like Carrothead's been bothering me."

"More like the other way around. He's constantly coming up behind me and scaring me."

"Actually, it is more like catching you talking to yourself," Perry said as he walked out of the room behind where Grae was standing.

"And he's done it again," Grae grumbled. "Maybe we could trade siblings."

"Oh, you would give Carrot back after she'd worshiped at the altar of SpookyWorld for a few days."

Grae laughed. It felt good to feel slightly normal for a few moments.

Gav continued to chat about Carrie's latest antics and how the recent weather kept him from getting to work for two days. As Grae listened, she walked toward the closet where she had found her grandmother's papers. The door was cracked open and she could see a small manila envelope wedged between the door frame and the floor. Grae bent down and pulled at the envelope. A piece of the flap tore off in her hand and she noticed the old glue on the back, it was still sticky. She pulled at it again and a key fell out.

"So, I was wondering if you thought any more about the prom," Gav asked.

Grae turned her attention away from the key and started pacing again. "Oh, yeah, that would be great. When is it again?"

"Ah, I think it's the second Saturday in May. What's your favorite color?"

"My favorite color, why?"

"Just answer the question."

"It's purple, dark purple." Grae noticed that the front door was open, which was unusual considering the weather. Something small and furry darted across the porch.

"I think they make cummerbunds in purple. I will wear purple."

"You don't necessarily wear one that is my favorite color. It needs to match my dress."

"What color will your dress be?"

"I don't know." Grae walked to the door and looked to see if she could see the animal.

"Don't girls usually buy clothes in their favorite color?"

"Well, yes, sometimes, but not…"

"I'll be wearing a purple cummerbund. I wonder how you spell that."

"T-H-A-T."

"Oh, she's not only smart and pretty, but she's funny too."

Grae stopped pacing and looked in the large mirror that hung in the foyer.

"Hate to have to run, but I've got to get ready for work. Maybe we will be back in school by Monday. I sure hope so. This stuff has got to melt so we can start baseball practice."

"Yeah, I'm ready for spring."

"Me too! Okay, well, talk to you later."

"Okay, have fun at work." Grae heard a click. As she turned off the phone, she looked at herself in the mirror. "He said I was pretty."

"Well, you are, sugarplum. Anyone can see that." Grandpa Mack came from the back of the house. "Now, that young man said his last name was McGavock."

"Yes, his name is James McGavock, but everyone calls him Gav. Do you know his family?"

"Darling, everyone knows his family. It's one of the oldest families in Southwest Virginia. They used to be one of the richest too, and I guess they still are to a certain extent, but these days no one is as rich as they used to be."

"Yes, we know all about that."

"Well, I guess you do." Grandpa took off his boots and set them down at the end of the hallway.

"I want to show you something, Grandpa." Grae walked over to the closet. She straddled the doorway as she knelt down to pick up the key. All of a sudden she had that weird moving feeling again and her vision began to fuzz and go dark. She stumbled and Grandpa caught her. Once he sat her down in the hallway, she felt fine again. It was as if someone had a switch to turn this strange feeling on and off.

"Are you okay? Feeling strange again?" Grandpa knelt down beside her.

"I think I'm okay. I wanted to show you something." She had dropped the key on the floor when that feeling hit her. She reached and picked it up. It felt cold in the palm of her hand. "This key, I found it in the closet with Granny's research stuff. Do you know where it came from?"

Grandpa Mack took the key out of Grae's hand, and his kneeling position quickly changed to him sitting on the floor next to her. He turned the key over and over in his hand and let out a big sigh before answering. "This key came from a long, long time ago."

"Does it have something to do with the Mansion?"

"Not exactly, but it has been in our family for a very long time."

Grae looked puzzled. "Why would a key stay in the family? What does it open?"

Grandpa Mack took off his John Deere cap and rubbed his head. Grae could see small brown patches around the edges of his hairline. It was the signs of a life of working in the sun. "If it was up to me, this key would have been destroyed years ago. All it has brought in my lifetime is heartbreak." He handed it back to Grae. "But your grandmother wouldn't hear of it. She said there was always hope if we kept the key." Grandpa stood up, his bones popping with each level he rose until he was standing straight. "Where's your hope now, Belle?"

Grae remained seated and watched her grandfather as he put his cap back on and walked toward the front door. He seemed to be so far away, in another time. She thought he was going to walk outside, but as he turned and walked back to her, she remembered that he didn't have his boots on. "You can keep that key, Grae, if you want. But do not let your mother know you have it. Seeing it would hurt her very much, and she doesn't need any more hurt. Are we straight?"

"Yes, Grandpa. I'm sorry."

"Darling, don't be sorry. Your grandmother put it there for someone to find. Maybe someday I can gather up the strength to tell you the story, but not right now. Sometimes the truth has to wait." He turned and walked back toward the kitchen. "What I wouldn't give to trade a cup of regret for a pound of prevention."

After he left, Grae began to examine the key more closely. It was unlike any key she had ever seen before. She presumed it was a skeleton key, as its sleek long design favored a body of bones. There were swirls and curls in the head of the key. It was very fancy and creative in the way the heavy metal had been sculpted. It reminded her of the Mansion, an ornate design to the outside, but it lead to a simpler use from within. The key was probably shiny brass in its early life, but now was tarnished and dark with an edge of corrosion in the corners of the swirls and the sharp edged cutouts that met an ancient lock.

She thought about the life the key had, where it had been, who had owned it. She wondered why it was so important to her grandmother and so hurtful to her mother. She would honor her grandfather's wishes and not allow her mother to know she had it. She couldn't chance leaving it in her room. Perry might be snooping, or her mother might come upon it as she put Grae's clothes away. Worse still, Clara might decide to place it somewhere obvious, if she decided to make her presence known again.

Grae went up to her bedroom, looking carefully around upon her entrance. She didn't know what she expected to see, but she was afraid that from now on she would always be expecting something. She opened her jewelry box that she had in the nightstand next to her bed. It was a box of treasures that contained many things, but very little jewelry.

Near the bottom right hand corner there was one of her baby teeth that the tooth fairy failed to collect. It was from a night when her parents fought and no one checked her pillow. A friendship bracelet was on top of it. It was multicolored pastel beads and Melinda Ellison had given it to her. They had been best buds. Two weeks later, her family moved away rather suddenly. She often wondered what had happened to her.

On the left side of the box was a collection of ticket stubs from concerts and Broadway shows she had seen. It was an eclectic variety from hard rock to country to classic musicals and everything in between. It was one of her father's favorite activities, and they had gone to several each year for as long as she could remember. It was one family activity that she would miss. Everyone seemed happy on those trips.

There were dozens of other small items in the box, but what Grae was searching for was a small red velvet bag. Inside it was an antique gold chain that her Granny Belle had given her when she turned 13. It was very unusual in its design. The links in the chain were several different sizes, but all fit together perfectly. Granny had told her that it was a good example of how everyone didn't have to be just alike to exist together. Grae smiled remembering her Granny's aged hands as she handed the chain to her. "I will give you another special gift when you turn 18 and it will change your life." Grae wondered what it would have been. Her grandmother would not see her on her 18th birthday.

Despite the variety of sizes of the links, the key fit over them and looked perfect on the chain. Grae decided that the best way to keep her mother from knowing about it was to hide it in plain sight. She would wear the chain under her shirt. After she had it on for a couple of days, her mother would not think anything about it. She could also put it in her pocket, if necessary. She slipped the chain over her head and laid the key next to her skin. So many weird things had been happening to her lately, she didn't know what to believe. But, there was warmth from that key, like the metal held years of power from all those who had used it.

EIGHT

The temperatures rose and the snow melted quickly. By Monday, road conditions improved and school was back in session. Kat dropped Grae and Perry off at the high school. She had a job interview mid-morning for a counselor position in the financial aid department at the local community college. It wasn't exactly the use of her education as she had once dreamed; but it would be a great way to get her foot in the door, and the salary and benefits would go a long way to begin a new life.

It seemed like a lifetime, instead of a week, since Grae had been in school. So many things had happened to her that she hardly thought she was the same person.

"Hey, Grae!" Like clockwork, Carrie appeared. "It was cool having a week off, but I was ready to come back. It's boring at home, and I missed you."

"Hi, Carrie, yes, I was ready to come back to school too. It's too secluded at the Mansion."

"I bet! But it is such a cool place." Carrie continued to walk with Grae. "I've been doing some thinking about the After Prom party. You know, I am on the committee. During study hall, I want to tell you some of my ideas, okay?"

"Sure, I'm not much of a party planner though. But my mom is really good at that kind of stuff."

"Oh, that's great! Because one of my ideas might really need her help." Carrie took her bubbly self on down the hallway, and Grae made her way to her locker.

"I still don't think you gave me an answer about the prom." Grae turned to see Gav standing behind her. "So, I thought I would start with something smaller. I'm off on Friday night. Would you like to go to the movies?" Grae smiled. He was persistent.

"What kind of movie did you have in mind?"

"Are you playing hard to get, or are you this evasive with everything?" Gav leaned on the locker beside hers. "We can see any movie playing at the theatre that you would like to pick. Ladies choice, I will even include animation."

"Well, who could turn an offer like that down?"

"That still wasn't an answer. It was another question."

"The answer is yes, James McGavock. My grandfather says you come from a famous family. How could I turn down Virginia royalty?"

Gav started laughing. "Oh that is funny. I look forward to meeting this man." The bell rang. "Can I walk you to class?"

"That would be delightful."

"Okay, so here is my idea." Carrie barely waited for Grae to sit down in study hall before she began talking. "We were trying to come up with really cool things to do for After Prom. In the past, there have been like games or movies or stuff like that. But I was thinking it would be really cool to have it at the Mansion."

Grae had really only been half listening until that point. She was trying to work on her calculus homework. "What?"

"Just hear me out. There's all that property and that big stage, and I wasn't thinking about a full-fledge SpookyWorld, just maybe parts of it and some music and stuff." Carrie stopped talking and stared at Grae. "You don't like the idea." Carrie looked like a sad first grader that wasn't allowed to go trick-or-treating.

"Well, I just don't know. I mean, you know the owner, he might not like it. It would be all night and that might be hard, and it would probably be expensive."

"Oh, the junior class has raised a lot of money. All our fundraisers were really successful. We could pay for use of the property and decorations and food. You had said before that your mom planned lots of events when you all lived in Charlotte. Didn't you say that she catered some of the parties at your house?"

Grae should have known better than to talk about the past. It always got her in trouble. "Well, I guess I could ask my mom and grandfather, and they could talk to the owner." Carrie's face lit up. "Now, I'm not making any promises. It might be a lot of liability, too."

"Oh, one of our committee members' father owns an insurance agency, and she's already asked him about getting insurance for the event, wherever it is held."

Grae shook her head; Carrie had thought of everything.

"Carrie says that the junior class has raised a lot of money." When Grae got home that afternoon, she had found her mother and grandfather in one of the barns on the property. Her grandfather also oversaw the livestock, and his main foreman was out for a month with surgery. No one else knew the animals as well as Grandpa Mack. There was about to be a birth in the barn and that meant he would be spending a lot of time there that night.

"I don't know what Josiah would think about having an all-night party here." Grandpa Mack was stroking Jezebel's mane, soothing her as she had been in labor for some time. This would be her second colt and might become a new project for Perry. Grandpa was determined to make him into a farm hand this summer, despite the fact that Perry wanted to get a real job as he had told his grandfather.

"Now, don't be so hasty, Dad. This might work out to be a good thing. He's been looking for ways to raise revenue. He's built so many things for the other events that have been held here. It would be a great way to get some more young volunteers acquainted with the property for SpookyWorld." Kat had told the owner, when he agreed to let her live there, that she would assist with any event planning he wanted her to do. She had been involved in many school and civic events in Charlotte, and she knew how to run a committee to be less on bureaucracy and more on activity.

Grae smiled as she saw a little of that mother she knew. Given a focus, there wasn't much that she couldn't make happen. The idea of having the After Prom party on the Mansion property hadn't thrilled her at first, but she saw a spark in her Mom that gave her hope. It would also make Carrie very happy, and Grae was starting to realize that Carrie really was her friend.

The owner, Josiah, agreed to the After Prom party idea if Kat would oversee it. With less than two months to organize, she began meeting with the teacher representatives and the After Prom committee. It was quickly decided that there would be a low scale SpookyWorld on the grounds, a band on the main stage, and the lower floors of the Mansion would be set up as game rooms. The General Store building and a huge tent in the backyard between the house and the stage would be where the food was served.

Seniors were not on the After Prom committee, as it was purely a junior class project. This did not disappoint Grae in the slightest as it gave her more time to explore the property and read her grandmother's research. She was becoming increasingly more intrigued by the history of the property and those who had lived there.

As March and its winter scape left and April progressed to spring, Grae and Perry began taking walks after school across the many acres of land. Kat had gotten the job she applied for at the community college, so they had a couple of hours after school before she came home from work. It wasn't long before Grandpa Mack got a John Deere Gator out for them to explore in. Riding around in this utility vehicle, that Grae called a country golf cart, made their explorations quicker. Cedar Run Creek ran across the property. Its waters were old with history and young with life. On the creek banks was a carpet of ferns, green and lush, with wild irises popping up in clusters. Their buds were golden yellow like a farm fresh egg yolk or purple like the wild phlox that seemingly grew everywhere.

They followed roadbeds that their grandfather and his friends created in their youth and explored the highs and lows of the land. Perry chipped away at the giant boulders and took home long flat sections of red, blue and gold slate. His agriculture teacher was amazed at the variations of color and rewarded Perry with some much needed extra credit. Grae picked water cress for her mother's salads and bouquets of spring wildflowers to sit in Mason jars in the room of glass. Days passed and weeks went by with no evidence of Clara or any other strange occurrences.

Sometimes on their outings, Grae would take her homework and sit by the creek. She found an old map of the land that showed family cemetery locations. On a long Saturday morning, Perry used his newly learned compass skills to locate one of the cemeteries. It was about two miles from the Mansion, and they had to park the Gator and walk part of the way. They were disappointed to find only one stone. Only a few of the words on it were legible, Baker and 1786.

"Baker, isn't that the name of the man that was murdered in the Mansion?" Perry asked as he knelt by the stone with a paper and pencil to make a rubbing. For some reason, making rubbings had become a new hobby of Perry's. The week earlier when they had been off on a Friday for Easter break, Perry had gone with Kat to work so he could walk to a nearby cemetery and make rubbings. With those he had taken from a cemetery down the main road from the Mansion, he was close to having a three-ring binder full of them.

"Joseph Baker was his name, but he wasn't murdered in the Mansion. The murder occurred on the property, but the Mansion didn't exist then."

"Then where did he live?"

"He built a cabin on the property. Legend has it that the first part of the Mansion was built around it."

"Which part is that? I don't remember seeing any walls with logs."

"If it's true, they have probably been covered up years ago by other types of walls. I don't know if Grandpa knows anything about it or not." Grae knelt down beside the Baker grave. As she looked over the horizon, she saw something shimmer in the light on the next hill over. "Let's go over there," she said, pointing to the north.

It was hard going down the hill. There were several large holes in the hillside. Grandpa had warned them about watching where they walked. He told them there were caves all over the property and that after a very wet winter, like they had just experienced, there might be some areas that might open up into the caves. The property also had over 30 springs throughout and was located on a fault line. All of these things made the old ground rather unstable in places.

When they finally reached the area Grae had seen the glimmer coming from, she couldn't find anything shiny, but did notice that the ground seemed to have two large humps side by side.

"I wonder if someone could be buried under there," Perry said. "This might be some sort of cemetery."

As Perry walked around the area looking for similar places, Grae sat down on one of the humps, exhausted from the climb. She fingered the chain around her neck, picking up the key and running it back and forth. Her vision started blurring and everything around her began to tilt. She put her hands down on each side of her to steady herself. Just as quickly as it had started, the feeling left her. She looked up to find her brother standing over her.

"Grae, I think you should come over here with me and see this."

"Grandpa, we found these stones and they were lying on their sides. Some of them looked like tombstones, others just like rocks. Most didn't have any writing left on them except maybe a letter or a number. Are they graves?" Perry sat across from his grandfather at the dinner table. Kat seemed preoccupied until Perry's last question.

"Graves? You've found graves. What have you two been doing?" Their mother didn't seem at all happy with this development.

"Mom, we were just exploring." Grae touched her mother's hand. "Perry was looking for that old cistern that Grandpa told him about. Perry's Ag teacher is curious about it and told Perry it would make a good report. Grandpa thinks that it once piped water into the Mansion."

"Yeah, I thought if I could find it, I would draw a map showing how it might have worked," Perry added.

"So, while he was looking, I was digging up some wild flowers to plant in your flower bed. We were in that grove of trees on top of the hill behind the house. The stone was only partially visible, but after we dug around it a little we could see some writing."

Grandpa took another bite. "This is mighty fine meatloaf! We can have this every week if you want," Grandpa smiled. His daughter still had a stern look. Grandpa continued, "Kids, people have lived on this land for three hundred years and there weren't always public cemeteries or church graveyards. So people were placed on their own land and generations of families would be buried together. This property wasn't always kept up by paid workers like your grandpa. Slaves worked this land for at least a hundred years, and when they died, they were most likely buried here too. There are bound to be generations of people buried here, free and slave."

"The name Baker was on one of the stones we found. Would that be the man that was murdered?" Grae asked.

"Well, Joseph Baker was the original man to set up a homestead here, or the first one we know about. He died in 1786."

"It seemed like it was somebody important. It looked like it might have been a fancier kind of tombstone. The other stones were smaller, like they might have been for children," Perry said. "Over on the hill next to where those graves were there was another area where we saw depressions in the ground, sunk in places. Some of them had rocks around them, like they had been placed. There were sunk -places too, but they looked strange, didn't look like graves."

"Those places are there because the coffins were made of wood and were put straight into the ground. Through the years, they deteriorated and collapsed and the soil above settled. They were probably slave graves. Those who were left behind probably filled those depressions in from time to time, but once slavery was over, they would have gone unattended. "

"Could some of those graves hold Bob and Sam?" Grae asked. "They are the ones who killed Joseph Baker."

"That's what the legend says." Grandpa took a big drink of milk. "But I don't believe it."

"But they were tried in court and convicted of the murder. I read all about it in Granny's papers."

"It wouldn't have been the first or last time that innocent men were convicted of crimes."

"So you think that they were innocent?" Perry was really getting into the conversation. Grae looked over at her mother; she was getting paler and paler.

"I think that there wasn't any such thing as an accident when it came to a master and his slaves. Those that served on that jury were white men, land owners in this community. A white man was dead and someone was going to have to pay."

"How would anyone ever find out the truth?" Perry asked. Kat had stood up and started collecting the dishes.

Grae stood up to help her mother. "They wouldn't, Perry, well, short of going back in time." Grae had barely finished the sentence when she heard the sound of dishes breaking. Everything that Kat had in her hands was now on the wooden floor.

NINE

April faded into May and the After Prom preparations were in the final stages. Much to Carrie's delight, a zombie theme was chosen to go along with the mini SpookyWorld activities. She had also convinced Kat to carry that theme over into the food and was thrilled at her creativity.

Grae wasn't overly excited about having the junior and senior class to her home for a gigantic non-sleepover, but she humored Carrie as much as she dared.

"Don't worry, Grae, nothing will be bad. Everything will be ghoul." Carrie's bubbly habits had transformed into her own sarcastic spooky humor. Grae was sure that Gav must be ready to kill Carrie.

Grae saw Gav every day at school, and they went out usually whatever weekend night he was off. But spring was all about baseball and track, and Gav excelled at both of them. Being talented in all sports meant that the college scholarship offers were already pouring in.

"I've been meaning to ask you what colleges you've applied to," Gav asked one evening as he and Grae ate dinner after watching a movie. "That might influence which college I decide on." There it was again, that smile. Grae knew it would get her into trouble one day.

"Well, I have applied to a few, but I will probably end up going to community college."

"Oh, I guess I thought since you are so smart and all that, you would be going away to a four-year school. Not that there's anything wrong with…"

"Well, that's another thing that changed when my father went to prison." Grae set her fork down and looked out the window. They had gone to an early movie at the local multiplex and the sun was now slowly setting. The sun was red, like fire. Her grandfather had told her once that a red setting sun was the sign of a hot day following.

Gav reached over and touched her hand. "Grae, you don't have to talk about this if you don't want to."

At what point does a young girl fall in love? Is it an accumulation of many things over a period of time, a thousand little heart flutters that add up to an explosion of emotion? Or is it one exquisite moment that just instantly warms her heart? This would be the moment Grae would remember for the rest of her life.

"It's okay. I don't mind talking to you about it." Grae picked up her fork again and twirled it around and around in her spaghetti. "My parents had big plans for me to go to some really great school. Perry and I both had hefty college funds. But the government seized them. They ruled that it wasn't our money." Grae paused and looked up. Gav was watching her intently with understanding eyes. "We basically came here with nothing. I'm not sure what would have happened to us if we didn't have Grandpa."

"I'm sorry. I knew some of the story, but I had no idea that it was…"

"This bad? Yeah, we were homeless. I think there is still more debt out there, but the judge did something to attach it to my father and keep my mother out of it. She sort of started over with a clean slate. Only problem is that she stayed home and raised us and didn't build a career. So she's got an education, but no experience."

"That's how we will be in a few years."

"It's going to be hard for her, but she is strong, and she's already starting to build a new career." Grae laid down the fork again and pushed the plate away. She had played enough. "I guess I'm going to have to figure out another way to get my education, but I don't mind. People who work hard for things appreciate them more."

"That is very true. I know that hard work and practice is the reason why I have done so well in sports." Gav leaned over the table. "And I will let you in on a secret. Everyone thinks that the McGavocks are so wealthy. Well, once upon a time they were. But if it wasn't for my athletic scholarships, I would have to get a whole bunch of student loans. I have two older sisters, one got an athletic scholarship and the other one owes her soul to the bank. My parents helped them as much as they could, but raising four kids is hard these days. Mom was a partner in a law firm, but after she got sick, she had to cut back to just a few hours a week. Her medical bills were a heavy hit."

"Is your mother okay now?" Grae realized that neither Gav nor Carrie talked much about their mother. She had only met her once and would describe her as frail with all of Carrie's redheaded features.

"She had breast cancer, twice. She's been cancer free for almost two years now, but she's never really gained all her strength back." Gav folded his napkin into the shape of a small triangle. "It worries us. The doctor says that having cancer twice in five years and all the treatments that went with it takes a lot out of a person."

"I would say so. But two years cancer free is great!" Grae enjoyed having this conversation with Gav. Sometimes by sharing the bad stuff, you learned a lot of the good stuff, too.

It was starting to get dark, and Gav told her that he had to travel to an out-of-town baseball game very early the next morning. As they were driving home, their conversation drifted to the prom.

"I still don't know what color your dress is. How am I going to buy your flowers?"

"The same way you got your cummerbund."

"That was sneaky telling Carrie, so she could tell Mom what to order. I just don't understand what the big secret is."

"It will just be a surprise." They turned down Major Graham Road. Off in the distance, a bright, almost full, moon shined down. It gave an illusion of mystery to the night. Gav pulled through the large ornate metal gates and drove up the driveway. As they got out of the car and walked across the lawn, they saw movement in the back of the house.

"Y'all have a cat?" The small animal seemed to be chasing something.

"It's the farm cat. His name is 'The General.'"

Gav laughed, "Guess that means he is in charge. It's hard to see him; what does he look like?"

"He's all black except for white paws. He has large green simian eyes and a crooked tail with the tip missing. He just seems to appear in places. I think he is a one-cat army. He doesn't seem to like people much, except Grandpa."

By this point, they were standing at the door. This was the first time they experienced an end-of-date encounter on a dark porch. In this light, Gav seemed to tower over Grae. She felt very small standing next to him.

"You know, I was thinking that our first kiss would be on prom night, but somehow that moon is telling me something different." Grae noticed that Gav looked so relaxed and comfortable with the situation. Perhaps he had lots of experience giving first kisses on porches. "Contrary to popular opinion, I've not had many girlfriends, and no one like you."

Grae's nervousness miraculously left her as Gav leaned down. She would have to remember to thank the moon later.

TEN

Grandpa Mack hired a crew of extra workers that weekend to tackle a list of sprucing up chores, as he called them, in preparation for the following weekend's events. The property was bustling with activity inside and out. Grae and Kat spent all day Saturday cleaning the downstairs rooms.

"How will we ever get all these rooms cleaned today?" It was just after lunch and they had barely finished two rooms to her mother's satisfaction. There was really no time for her mother's obsessive-compulsive cleaning behavior to be in full swing.

"What we don't get done today, you will get done tomorrow, while the committee and I are picking up the catering supplies in Charlotte." Kat had a friend with a catering business. She had helped her friend by writing three successful grants for the friend's favorite charity, so now Kat called in a favor and was borrowing some equipment.

"Oh, Mom, but I was going to go exploring tomorrow."

"Whose prom is this? Whose friend wanted to have the party here?"

"Okay, okay, I surrender." The cleaning continued. Grae watched her mother's unrelenting determination to make everything sparkle as much as possible. Kat had always been used to keeping a new home immaculate, so working on a home as old as this was difficult. There were nooks and crannies with ancient dirt in them. It almost seemed as though the dust came back after they had finished a room, like the former occupants that legend said roamed the halls.

Grae worshipped her bed that night, after taking the longest shower of her life. Even afterward, she kept feeling like there were spiders crawling on her. As tired as she was, sleep did not come quickly. She watched as an ever-brightening moon glowed through the crack she left in the shutters. It continued to amaze Grae how blue the walls were in this room, even in darkness. While she imagined that they had probably been other colors through the years, the blue seemed to have become part of the soul of the room.

Out of the corner of her eye, she saw something move. She turned over on her left side and looked more intently. Something shiny was rolling on the floor. She reached over to her nightstand and retrieved a flashlight. Shining the light in that direction, she saw a red ball. It was the type of ball that you saw in big bins at a department store, hundreds of them in different colors. The ball was so lightweight that it didn't make a sound, but the movement could be seen nonetheless. Grae had noticed the ball in the corner of the left closet when she moved in, but really hadn't thought much about it.

Grae got up and turned on the lamp on her bedside table. The ball stopped moving. She looked to see if perhaps there was a breeze coming through the window or down the chimney, but neither the curtain nor anything else in the room was moving. It was hot, the air was still. She turned the light off again and got back into bed. A few minutes later, the ball resumed its movement, this time going in the opposite direction. "It's time to go to sleep, Clara." The ball stopped moving and all was still.

The next morning, a Sunday, Kat and her After Prom crew left at seven for their day long excursion to Charlotte to gather equipment and supplies. Perry and Grandpa also left early for a rare day of fishing on the New River. Grae was left alone at the Mansion to clean the foyer and the staircase, and to work on a ten-page report that was due on Wednesday.

Armed with a bucket of Murphy's Oil Soap, a scrub brush and a bunch of her Grandpa's old cotton undershirts, Grae began working on the staircase. Step by step, she scrubbed the wood. While her mother cleaned every week, it had been a long time since the steps and floor had received a real scrubbing, and Grae was amazed at the beauty of the wood. One task that Kat had promised the owner she would begin soon was stripping the floors and refinishing. It would be a laborious duty, but Grae could see that it would result in bringing new life to the old rooms.

By the end of the morning, she'd worked her way down the entire staircase and was pleased with the shine that the mid-day sun made. She fixed herself a tuna salad sandwich and went and sat in the room of glass. The weather would soon be too warm to sit in there for long, but Grae enjoyed how she could look out from all sides and see around the property.

She gazed down at the old brick building to the right. It was the old slave quarters from the time when the Graham family had lived there. Grae imagined there were many stories associated with it. She wondered about those that lived there and how hard their lives had been. She couldn't imagine all of the things they must have done just to survive.

Her thoughts then moved to a time even further back when the slaves of the Bakers worked the land. They probably just lived in a small log cabin, perhaps on the same area as this brick building. She wondered about Bob and Sam and their families. From all that she had read, she couldn't help but agree with Grandpa. There was something about that murder that didn't add up. Had they really intentionally murdered their master or did something else happen that led to Joseph Baker's death?

She finished her sandwich and got ready to begin cleaning the foyer. Her mother had asked that she also clean out the closet so that it could be used for last minute storage on prom night. She knew that there were a couple more of her grandmother's boxes of research in there, and her mother said she could take those boxes upstairs to her room.

From the hallway, Grae reached into the back of the closet and pulled out the two old umbrellas that she saw previously. She opened the one with the ornate handle and saw the beautiful green calico design. As she tried to close it, she heard a little rip in the fabric.

"Mom used to say it was bad luck to open an umbrella inside," Grae said out loud to herself. She leaned the old black umbrella on the wall behind her, unopened. On the right hand side of the closet, she saw the old stick vacuum cleaner and pulled it out.

She reached further into the middle of the closet to take out the two remaining boxes of documents and got that sick feeling again as she tugged the last one out. "I really must be allergic to something in here." As she regained her bearings, her hand went to the key on the chain around her neck. Her mother hadn't noticed Grae wearing it. "Maybe there is something in this closet that this key will open."

Out of the corner of her eye, she saw something red to the far left. Now that the boxes were out of the way, she could see that it looked like a piece of old wallpaper still attached to the wall. Still fingering the key, Grae walked inside to see it up close. As she reached toward the red, everything began to spin. A shrill sound filled her ears. She covered them with both hands and then realized that the horrible sound was coming from inside her head. Everything began to tilt and Grae felt herself falling. Something was pulling at her, from the outside, from the inside, like an unseen force was tearing her apart. She reached for the sides of the closet, but they were not there. She saw swirls of green and purple mist all around her. The air smelled stale like a damp basement. Her mouth tried to let out a scream, but it was silenced by the ever-increasing shrieking in her ears and the incredibly fast movement that was encircling her. Just as she felt a horrible sickness in her stomach creep up into her throat, everything went black.

ANOTHER TIME

ELEVEN

"Oh, gosh, it feels like I am lying on a bed of rocks." Grae opened her eyes and realized she was, in fact, lying down. She slowly raised her head and pushed her body up to a sitting position. Looking around her, she saw that the ground she was lying on was covered in rocks of varying shapes and sizes. "What are all those rocks doing in…?" Grae stopped short of finishing the sentence as she looked around herself more closely. "This isn't the foyer of the Mansion. I'm outside on the ground." She looked down at herself. "Oh, this must be some kind of dream, maybe I passed out. This isn't what I was wearing."

Grae's jagged cut-off denim shorts and double tank top were gone. She was wearing a long brown wool skirt; it was tattered at the edges and looked as if it hadn't been washed in months. Her shirt was a lighter fabric with long sleeves. It might have once been white, but now it had a stained grey look to it. It was simply made with several buttons at the top, a couple of them hung as if literally by a thread ready to drop at the first slight breeze. Her feet were bare and dirty, no color on her toes. Grae reached for her neck. The key was still there, but the chain was now old worn leather.

Grae studied her surroundings more carefully. She was sitting on what appeared to be a well-worn path or road. The land was flat for about a hundred feet all around her with tall trees and short bushes every twenty feet or so in no particular order. In the distance, she could see rolling hills and wooded areas. There was not a building or a person in sight.

"You can't just stay there, sitting on the road," a voice said. It seemed to have come from a cluster of bushes about fifteen feet away from her.

"Who said that? Show yourself." Grae stood up and looked all around her. As if by instinct, her body took a crouched pose with her arms out in front of her, ready to fight the unknown.

A cat walked out of the bushes. Grae looked at it intently; she had seen that cat before. She watched behind it for someone to follow its path.

"Do you always talk to yourself when you're alone?" the voice asked.

"Oh, great! Now that sounds like something Perry would say." She threw her hands up in the air. "Okay, little brother, come on out, and bring your friends with you. This is really an elaborate joke you've played. I don't care what Mom says, I'm going to kill you."

"I'd be careful what I said if I was you. A wish can turn into regret faster than you can imagine," the same voice said.

"Who is talking? That's not Perry's voice. Come on out."

"I'm right here in front of you."

"What? All I see is a cat and it looks like The General."

"Yes, I am a cat, presently."

"Ha! Ha! Very funny, jokes over. I need to get back to the Mansion and finish cleaning before Mom gets home."

"The Mansion isn't there."

"What? Stop talking crazy. What do you mean 'the Mansion isn't there?' Did something happen? How long was I passed out?" Grae rubbed her head and looked around. "Please come out so I can see you, I'm tired of talking to this cat."

"Well, get used to it, you are going to be talking to 'this cat' for quite some time. 'This cat' is going to save your life."

Grae knelt down in front of the cat. "I must be hallucinating. Something really bad must have happened to me, and they took me to the hospital and gave me lots of drugs."

"You are not hallucinating." From this vantage point, it almost looked like the cat's mouth was moving. "You've travelled a long way. Not geographically, but through time."

"I'm sitting down. I surrender. I think I will just let the drugs kick in."

"You still don't believe that it is the cat that is talking." The cat paced back and forth in front of Grae. "Okay, tell the cat to do something. Give it a command of your own choosing."

Grae shook her head. "Walk to the right." The cat walked to Grae's right. "Well, that could just be coincidence, it was pacing anyway."

"Give a harder command." The cat sat down in front of her as if it was waiting for something.

"Turn around in a circle." The cat walked around in a circle and sat back down. "Lay down." The cat laid down on its side. "Roll over."

"I am not a dog. Will you stop with the canine commands?"

"You certainly have the temperament of a cat." Grae stood up again. "What am I doing? You are a cat and you are not talking to me. I am leaving now. Maybe I can walk this hallucination off." Grae turned and began walking toward the wooded area nearby.

"Stop! You can't go off by yourself walking through the woods."

"I've been looking around. I've got my bearings. I think the Mansion is in that direction." Grae pointed toward the woods. "Besides, this is probably all a drug-induced dream anyway." All of a sudden Grae felt the cat jump up on her back, its claws digging into her shoulders. She swung at it and it jumped back down.

"Girl, I will speak to you more directly." Grae had spun around and now faced the cat. "I am going to stand up on my hind legs. You must listen carefully to what I am about to say." The cat stood up on its hind legs. "You have travelled through time. The Mansion of which you speak is not where you know it because it does not yet exist. The year is 1786. You have travelled more than two centuries to reach here." The cat sat down again. "That is not a position that I care to stay in for very long. My days on two feet are long behind me."

"You are talking crazy. Travel through time, it's not possible."

"Oh, but it is, certain people have been doing it for as long as there has been time to travel in."

"Let's say for a moment that I believe that I am talking to a cat about time travel, which by the way I don't. Who are these certain people?"

"Well, legend tells us that there was a certain young woman who was a close personal servant of Queen Cleopatra. The woman was also Cleopatra's half-sister, and she spent many private hours with the Queen and learned of her great powers. Her name was Charmian and many of those powers also ran through her veins. Charmian died with her Queen, but not before she passed the powers onto her eldest daughter."

Grae sat engrossed in what the cat was saying. "What powers?"

"Queen Cleopatra had many powers that were bestowed upon her. Charmian's power was related to time and the ability to manipulate it. That power has been passed down through the ages and each generation must use it or it shall be lost."

"And what does that have to do with me?"

"It is now your generation. You are the chosen one of your generation to use this power to travel through time. It is up to you as to what you will use that power to discover."

"I am so ready for these drugs to wear off. I've really got a lot to do." Grae stood up and began to walk toward the woods again.

"I'm not going to warn you again. You need to be careful."

"Okay, what was your name again?"

"Well, you referred to me as 'The General.' I believe that name shall suffice for the time being."

"Okay, General, I'll keep going on with your little game. So you think I have descended from this Charmaine person."

"The name was Char-me-an."

"Char-me-an. So what makes you so sure?"

"Well, first off, you have the Sign of the Eyes." Grae looked at The General in confusion. "The irises of your eyes are each a different color. They are two different shades of blue." Grae reached to touch her eyeballs in search of her contact lenses and realized that they were gone.

"Where are my contact lenses?"

"The year is 1786. They have not been invented yet."

"I wear them to disguise the difference in color. Kids used to make fun of me."

"Children can be cruel. Your mother also was ridiculed because of that."

"Mom? Her eyes are the same color; they are a beautiful violet color. That's why I chose that color of lenses."

"So you chose to create an illusion that your eyes are the same color as your mother's, a rare color?" The General began to pace again, this time with his tail in the air. He seemed quite pleased with himself.

"Well, I never really thought about it, I guess." Grae scratched her head, and then formed herself into her safe ball position. "You mean my mother has travelled in time? That's impossible! She's never once been away from us for any length of time. We would know if she had been gone."

"Would you?"

Grae swore that The General now had eyebrows and one went up in a challenging manner.

"Your mother has a mark on the underside of her right wrist, does she not?"

"Yes, it's a birthmark. It looks like the infinity symbol. She always told me it was there to remind her that life was limitless. It was not bound by space or time. I told her that I wanted one too." Grae paused and pondered what she had just said.

"And how did she reply to that?" The General asked. He was now sitting close to her.

"She said, 'I don't want you to have one.'"

"Look at the underside of your right wrist."

Grae slowly turned over her wrist. She gasped as she saw the identical mark that was on her mother, the infinity symbol.

The General put his paws up on her knee. "Now, do you believe me?"

"I, I don't know what to think. Everything has been so strange lately, so confusing."

"Well, my dear, that's not going to change for a while, but you need to listen to me and allow me to help you on this journey. You have come here for a purpose, a mission of sorts. Soon you will discover what it is."

"I still don't know if I believe any of this, but this is slowly becoming more real than I want it to be. Assuming you are right and this isn't a hallucination, how will I ever get home?"

"That remains to be seen, you have to fulfill your mission first and you have to obey the rules of time."

"What are the rules of time?"

"The rules of time are many and varied and you will learn them, well, over time." Grae presumed it was a cat laugh she heard after he said that though she'd never heard one before. "The first rule you need to learn is to adapt. You need to adapt yourself to this present time period. You need to not stand out, not to be thought of as unusual, or out of place. Something dire and disastrous will happen if you are thought to have any unusual powers."

"What do you mean dire and disastrous?"

"Did you study about the Salem witch trials in history?"

"Yes."

"Some of those ladies were visiting from another time."

"Okay, I get it."

"Thankfully, there are a few things that are taken care of during the transformation journey."

"Transformation journey?"

"You have a habit of repeating things, don't you? I wouldn't do that with those you will be with soon. It will not work to your advantage." The General began walking down the road away from the woods. "The transformation journey was what occurred between your time and this time. You probably experienced a lot of strange sensations during that."

"I thought I was dying! It felt like I was being pulled apart from the inside out. Like something was inside my brain pulling it in different directions."

"Well, you traveled over 200 years. During transformation, everything is removed from you that does not belong in the time to which you are travelling. That's why you do not have the contact lenses in your eyes or any of your former clothing. You are clothed for today's time and in such a manner as befitting your role in this society."

Grae looked down at her attire. "So, I am poor and unfashionable in this time?"

"Actually, you are worse than poor. You are an indentured servant. You have nothing and have a debt against your future."

"I'm a slave?"

"No, a slave is owned. He or she is considered to be property. You are a servant. You owe a debt that must be paid off. Once that debt is paid, you are then free."

"Kind of like a mortgage in my time?" Grae smiled for the first time in this new world.

"Well, yes, I guess you could sort of liken it to that, only you must work off this debt in servitude."

"Lovely. This is kind of reminding me of being a teenager. Oh yeah, that's what I am, in both worlds."

"Well, it's hardly the same. But most indentured servants were under the age of 21. There are stories about some being as young as six years old and being servants until they turn 21."

"You mean I'm going to have to stay here until I am 21? Mom will freak out. She can't take that kind of stress. There's already been too much going on." Grae began to pace back and forth and pull on the key around her neck.

"Calm down." The General came back to where Grae was pacing. "Time will not pass while you are gone."

"What?"

"When you return, no time will have passed. It will appear as if you never left. You were alone when you transformed, correct?"

"Yes, how did you know?"

"That is the ideal situation and what I was hoping would happen. Transforming unnoticed is one of the rules of time."

"So you are sure that my mother will not know that I am gone?"

"As long as the rules of time are obeyed, no time should have passed."

"And what if a rule is not obeyed?"

"Remember what I said before, dire and disastrous."

"Has anyone ever become stuck in another time?"

"Yes."

"And what happened to that person?"

The General again walked down the path a short distance before turning back to Grae. "He was transformed into a cat."

"What? You?"

"Yes, it's a long story. We really need to get going and transition you into this time and life."

Not knowing what else to do, Grae began to follow him. "Hey, you said that all of the stuff from the previous time is removed. How come I still have this key?"

Without even turning around, The General answered, "It's from this time."

That piece of information surprised Grae. "Where are we going?"

"To the farm of Joseph Baker."

TWELVE

Grae followed The General down the long winding road. Grae's feet hurt as they hit small stones and pebbles. The weight of the clothes felt strange to her, but they were not as hot as she imagined. She thought perhaps it was because of the looseness.

She decided that silence was best for now. The General had revealed too much already and her mind was still jumbled. The dozens of questions that were bursting in her brain could not be silenced long though.

"Did my mother ever come back to this time period?" The General stopped and turned toward her.

"Yes, she did, twice."

"Why, wasn't once enough?"

"In her case, it was not."

"What was she trying to find?"

The General began walking again. At first, Grae thought that he was ignoring her.

"Redemption."

"I don't understand. Who needed redemption? Was it some mystery that occurred in this time?"

"No, she sought her own redemption."

"From what?"

"You will have to ask her that."

The path led through a cluster of trees and then blue sky shown like a welcome mat above them. On the hill a short distance away, Grae saw a log cabin. She gazed upon the structure. It looked as if it had literally sprung from the land around it.

"It looks so natural there," Grae said.

The General stopped and joined Grae in her viewing. "It should, everything that was used to build it has come from this land. Let's sit down here for a moment; you need to know a little about how you will be living."

Sitting down, the view changed somewhat, but Grae could still see the cabin on the hill. Somehow with The General's last words, it seemed more imposing to her.

"That is the cabin of Joseph Baker. He and his slave, Bob, built it with their own hands. That doesn't mean they went somewhere and bought materials and put it together, it means that everything that went into it came from this land, by their sweat." The General stretched out and swished his tail. "The foundation, granite stone, is carved out of the side of a hill nearby. It took them weeks to chisel out enough large pieces and make that sturdy foundation, and their horses put in many good days of work dragging them back to that location. Each one of those logs represents a cedar or locust tree that was cut down with an ax, and then the logs were hewn to the right size and shape. Notches were cut to fit the logs together at the corners."

"What was used to fill up the holes between the logs?" Grae was engrossed in the description and all the work that was entailed.

"That process was called chinking. It involved taking mud and materials like twigs, moss, paper or other things to fill the holes. It makes for a very sturdy structure."

"It actually looks a little larger than I expected."

"That's very observant. It is slightly larger. It also has a basement, which is rather unusual for this time. It was what Joseph and Bob built first and the family lived in it before the cabin was completed. It was also constructed of stone. Part of it, to the rear, actually has just a wooden floor over it. You can walk out the back door and out on to it. It's a cellar now. There is a trap door in the floor on the outside and when you open it, there is a stairwell into the basement." The General stood up again and began pacing.

"Hmm, that does sound unusual, a lot of work for a cellar."

"Well, unfortunately, it had other uses. When they first settled here, Joseph Baker bought a bunch of slaves from a man that was leaving the area. Most of the slaves were rather dangerous, and he ended up holding them prisoner in there until they could be taken to be sold elsewhere." The General sat down again. "It was a hard experience on Joseph. He had grown up with good slaves, like Bob and his family were. He didn't like what he had to do."

"That's an interesting part. Are there any other buildings up there?"

"There's a smaller log cabin in the back where the slaves live. There's a good size barn and a fenced corral for the animals." The General got up. "Okay, we've wasted enough time. When we reach the cabin, you are going to knock on the door and tell them you are the indentured servant they have been expecting. You were supposed to arrive a few days ago. You're going to have to make up a story as to why you are late. Remember to watch how you speak. Don't use modern terms. Speak simply and only when you are asked a question. You are a servant. Remember, you are also probably from England, so you will have a slight accent."

"I bet a North Carolina accent isn't what you have in mind."

"No, but just speak plainly. Remember that during this time period, most of those in America hadn't been here too long themselves. So just copy their speech patterns."

"Oh, I don't know if I can do this. Can't I just go back now? I'm scared."

"You cannot go back until you fulfill your mission. That's one of the rules."

"But what's my mission?"

"It will come to you in time. Make the best of the situation. Don't reveal when and where you are truly from. Remember what I said, dire and disastrous."

They had arrived near the front of the cabin. Grae was just about to ask The General another question when the cabin door opened.

"Who are you?" An average sized man, rather on the short side, stood in front of her. He was wearing brown pants and a brown shirt with brown suspenders. He looked very brown.

"I am the servant, sir."

"You were supposed to have arrived a week ago. When the wagon train came, they said you ran off. A warrant will soon be on your head." Joseph Baker looked sternly at Grae. "So should I have you put in shackles? Did you indeed run?"

"Well, I…" Grae shook with fear.

"Speak up, young girl, what say ye?"

"I did run from the wagon master," Grae stuttered, "b-but, I walked on to the Baker farm as best I could. I come to work my debt."

"Why did you run from the man? Did he beat you?"

"No."

"Why did you run then? It is against all decrees for you to do so." Joseph Baker paused. "Why then?" He was now yelling.

"When, when we stopped for the night..." Grae paused as she saw a woman coming out from behind Joseph Baker. Grae assumed this was his wife. The woman came toward her and placed her hand on Grae's arm.

"Tell him, it's your only hope. Tell what happened." Grae saw kindness in her eyes, understanding.

"When we stopped for the night, the wagon master he lied down with me. He were drunk with the whiskey, and he tried to take liberties with me." Grae sighed and bowed her head. She hoped that her junior year drama class had paid off.

"Aye, the man stole bottles from our own stock when he came here."

"I know I am but an indebted girl, bond to service for some years, but I am spoken for by a man in the new land. I must stay pure for our union." Grae felt like a ventriloquist dummy; she had no idea where all these words were coming from. "I must try."

"You are betrothed? Why then are you in servitude?"

"My parents, brothers and I were all scheduled for passage to the new land. But my parents, they got the typhoid. We were left with nothing. My brothers were taken to an orphanage, but I was too old. My uncle, a spiteful man, said he was to pay my passage to my intended, but he signed my servitude instead."

"What be the family name of your intended?"

Grae, still looking at the ground, searched her mind for a name that would be appropriate for the time period.

"Speak girl, tell us the name, or I will think you are lying."

Grae slowly raised her head, "McGavock."

"You have lost your mind. They will have you shipped off to some horrible place." The General was pacing in front of Grae as she waited outside the slave cabin. "Couldn't you have said some name like Smith or Jones? McGavock, just one of the most distinguished names in the region."

"How was I to know what names I could use? It's not like I had any time to prepare for this journey? I was cleaning out a closet."

"Just don't talk. Maybe you can fake a fever and tell them later you were talking out of your head." The General started walking off. "I'm exhausted."

"Where are you going?"

"To get some rest and find something to eat. Try not to get into any trouble while I'm gone."

"But you can't leave."

"Just do what you are told and speak as little as possible. You need to make friends with the slaves and that will not be an easy thing to do."

THIRTEEN

It became evident that Joseph Baker decided to believe Grae's story. According to the indentured servant papers, that had miraculously appeared in the pocket of her skirt, her name was Arabella Young and she hailed from Wiltshire, England. The papers listed her age as 17 and that her servitude would be for almost two years.

The family might eventually use her to work in the main cabin, a position that would allow her to live there as well; but for now, she would be staying in the slaves' quarters. It was almost the middle of the day and the female slaves were busy preparing a meal. There was a large pot over an open fire behind the main cabin, the women slaves were busy adding ingredients to the stew building within. They gave Grae the task of peeling and chopping potatoes.

"Girl, you know how to skin a tater?" The younger of the two women asked her. Grae shook her head. "Can't speak or you 'fraid?"

"I not 'fraid," Grae said cringing as she heard herself. She could almost hear a collected "tsk" from all the English teachers she had ever had.

"Maybe you think you better than us 'cause your skin ain't dark." The woman howled with laughter. "You be our slave now."

"Leave her be," the older woman said. "She be free in a few years, you always be a slave." The older woman looked Grae up and down and inspected her work. "You be small, but your hands be fast. We might make a weaver out of you. We needs to get busy and make coverings for the winter."

Grae smiled and the older woman smiled back. Grae saw that the woman's smile showed she was missing many teeth. Grae bowed her head feeling badly for the privileged life she led, including her regular dentist visits. "What your name? What you be called?"

"My given name is Arabella Young, but my family has called me Belle for as long as I can remember."

"Belle, that be a purty name. I be called Sal and this here is Aggie. She be my sista's daughter and about as mean as a rattlesnake." Sal laughed deeply and her whole body looked as if it laughed too. "Aggie be with me since her momma died when Aggie was a little 'un. Somehow we managed to stay together. I come here with the Missus, I be with her family a long piece, that why she let me keep Aggie close."

"She seems like a nice lady," Grae could tell that Aggie was watching her closely out of the corner of her eye.

"She's a fine woman and Massa Baker, he a good man, got a temper, but most men do. Keep him away from the 'shine and he be a better man."

"You 'bout done with the peelin'?" Aggie asked. Grae held out the bowl to her. "You chop 'em up now and throw 'em in the kettle. I not be doing your work. I go check on the bread." Grae watched as Aggie walked away. She had a stride like she was always in a hurry, even if she didn't have far to go.

"Don't pay her no mind. It just be her way. She grow up hard."

"What happened?"

"Her momma died givin' birth, having a baby of a white man, one of Missus Baker's daddy's hired men. They drown that sweet baby that very night. My sista close her eyes one last time." Sal wiped her eyes with the corner of her apron. She was a large woman, big boned, stout for work. Her skin was the color of dark honey and was smooth and shiny, not a wrinkle on her face. Her hair told her age or a hard life. It was salt and pepper, heavy on the salt.

"Aggie never have no daddy neither. He got killed in a logging accident. Me and Bob are her family."

"Is Bob your husband?" Grae was careful to only use names she had heard from them. She couldn't reveal what she already knew. The General's dire and disastrous warning kept ringing in her ears.

"Me and Bob been together our whole lives. Raised up together on Missus Baker's family farm. We jumped the broom when we were young. We be closer than husband and wife, we be one person." Sal stirred the big cast iron kettle of stew. Her big spoon looked more like a boat oar it was so big, but Grae presumed that deep kettle would be feeding a whole lot of hungry people come noontime.

For the rest of the morning, Grae did whatever tasks that Sal or Aggie presented her. She swept out the slaves' quarters and was amazed that the entire cabin wasn't much bigger than her blue room at the Mansion. She hung clothes on a long clothes line after Sal took them out of another big kettle of boiling water. Her hands were scalded by the time Aggie rang the meal bell.

Grae watched as men, black and white, walked toward the back of the cabin from all directions. It was planting time, and acres and acres of corn and wheat were already growing. The corn was a main ingredient for Joseph Baker's distillery business, as well as a staple to feed the animals. Both the corn and wheat would be made into meal and flour at the grist mill nearby.

Most of the white men stared at Grae as they passed her. She handed them tin cups filled with cold spring water after Sal had given them heaping bowls of stew. The black men, Negroes, never made eye contact with her. Grae wondered which one was Bob until she saw Sal come up behind the biggest man in the group.

"Belle, girl, this here be my man, Bob. He be the strongest man on this farm. That puny thing sitting next to him is Sam, he be Bob's sista's boy." Sal named off some others in the group, they were sitting on the ground next to the slaves' cabin. The white workers, including Joseph Baker, were sitting at a long makeshift table to the rear of the Baker cabin. Aggie was running back and forth taking them more stew or bread and some were drinking coffee or milk.

Bob was a very large man. It was obvious that he could work circles around some of the younger men. From what few words Grae heard him speak to Sal, it appeared that he might have had a little schooling at some point.

The meal was over, and Grae was helping Sal and Aggie clean up. Joseph Baker walked toward them. Grae kept her head down.

"Sal, this girl got any work in her?"

Sal watched Grae as she answered. "Yes, sir, I think she do, Massa Baker. I think she be a smart girl."

"Girl, what is your name again?" Joseph Baker stood close to Grae; she could smell the sweat of work on him. He was not a lazy man.

"My name is Arabella, but people call me Belle."

"Belle, can you read and write?"

"Yes, sir."

"Then I want you to see if you can teach old Sal here how to write her name. Can you do that?"

Grae looked Joseph Baker straight in the face. She wondered if this was a test as she knew that most slave owners didn't want their slaves learning anything but how to work harder. She didn't see anything in his face that led her to think he was not being truthful. Behind him, she saw Sal, shaking her head.

"Yes, sir. I can do that, just as you wish." Then Grae saw something that she could hardly believe.

A smile crossed Joseph Baker's face. "Sal is special to my wife and she wants her to have some learning. This is a hard life we lead out here. You are going to learn that. I can't give my wife many nice things, but I can try to give her some kindness now and then. You help me do that, and I will forget about you running off."

Grae nodded to Mister Baker and stepped back. Out of the corner of her eye she could see Sal, hands on hips, smiling a big toothless grin. "Ah, now, Massa Baker, you think ole Sal can learn something. This ole head done quit learnin' years ago."

"I hardly believe that and you know how when my Nannie gets something in her head, there is no shaking it. You better learn something or I'll be in trouble."

"Lawd, sir, we don't want that, we surely don't." Sal went back to what she was doing.

Grae wasn't sure, but it seemed like Sal was seasoning a big hunk of meat. After Mister Baker left, she walked over to where Sal was working. She was using the big makeshift table that the men had eaten on earlier as her work table. She had salt and pepper and several other powdered spices in front of her.

"What are you doing?" Grae asked.

"Girl, what do you know? I am seasoning this here meat so I can roast it on that fire over there." Sal pointed to the fire that had previously had the big iron pot of stew cooking over it. "I guess you don't know what this here meat is, do you?"

"Beef?"

"No, it be venison. You know where venison come from?"

Grae knew this one; her Grandpa Mack was a hunter. "Deer."

"Lawd, Aggie, there is hope for this young'un." Grae turned to see Aggie carrying a big sack of something over her shoulder.

"Now, we can see if she be as good at peeling sweet taters as she be at watching you." Aggie put the entire sack on Grae's feet. It was heavy enough to hurt, but she would not give Aggie the satisfaction. Grae got a knife and the biggest pan she could find, and she pulled the sack of potatoes over to a tree near the barn. Then she sat down, leaning next to the tree and went to work. She'd never seen so many sweet potatoes. There must have been the equivalent of four or five bags of white potatoes that her mother would buy in the store. But there wasn't any use in complaining, this was her life for the time being and she had to accept it. Off in the distance, she could see The General sitting on a tree stump watching.

The task gave Grae time to think. This morning, she was cleaning out a closet in the 21st century, now she sat on the same land over 200 years earlier. No one would ever believe her and she didn't blame them, she didn't believe it herself. She kept thinking that she would wake up and it would all be a dream. The reality was that what she was experiencing was beyond her wildest dreams. She looked around and realized that it was indeed a view that she recognized. The mountains and hills of the Blue Ridge were even a tad more beautiful when they were less touched by man's hand. There was no sound of an interstate highway off in the distance as there was in the present day. The air was clearer, the sky was bluer, and the sounds were of the noise of nature, not the noise of a modern world.

Still peeling the bottomless bag of potatoes, Grae spied a robin digging in the dirt for a bug or worm. Though she dared not ask, she wondered what the month and day were. It would appear to be early spring, she presumed sometime in April. Perhaps she could say that travelling on the ship and the wagon train confused her and she wondered what the date was.

As the afternoon progressed, Aggie would come every so often and take the sweet potatoes that Grae had peeled and move them to the table where Sal was still working. The venison was roasting on a spit over the fire. Sal would get up and turn it every half hour. The smell was making Grae very hungry.

"Aggie, go get the molasses and the nutmeg, and bring the butter too." Those ingredients sounded like Thanksgiving to Grae, and she wondered if today was a special occasion of some sort.

When finally she had completed the peeling task, she carried the last of the potatoes to Sal. Half of them were already cooking in a huge pot inside the main cabin on the hearth. The other half, Sal was now cutting into long slices.

"Now, girl, you can sew these taters for ole Sal."

Grae couldn't hide her confused look fast enough and her expression must have tickled Sal. "Sweet Jesus, you look like I's told you the sky was green. Don't tell me you folks don't sew no taters over there across the water." Sal paused and shook her head. "Oh, merciful Jesus, give me strength to learn this poor girl some useful doings. Never no man gonna marry you if you not know how to do things."

Sal then proceeded to show Grae what sewing the taters meant. Sal took a big sewing needle and threaded it with white thread, doubled. Making a knot at the end, then she sewed a couple of anchor stitches into the end of the slice of potato. She ran the needle in and out through the potato slice working her way to the opposite end, and then added another one. This made a chain of potatoes.

"You keep sewing until you get it as long as you has room to hang. We gonna hang these in the smoke house and they gets good and dry and also has that smoky flavor to them." Sal held up a string of sweet potatoes that was about three feet long. "In the winter, we take these off the string and soaks them in boiling water. They be as good as they are now."

Grae was amazed at how ingenious this was. Preserving food was hard in the 1700s, but people found ways to keep as much tucked away for winter months as they could.

That evening the scene was similar to what Grae saw at midday, except this meal Joseph Baker ate inside with his family. "You might think it strange that we prepare our food with the Massa's food. But that the way Massa wants it. He says we all work hard, we all eat hard. It sure does save me lots of work."

"Now, Sal, we don't eat the same as the Massa's family all the time," Aggie said. "Theys have special company and has fine food."

"That be the truth and so do we. Whens Bob kills rabbits on a Sunday afternoon, we not invite the Bakers to our table neither."

"I sure they are sad not to be eatin' our rabbits when they be eatin' their big fine Easter ham," Aggie said.

"Belle, let me tell you something, you needs to learn this. You don't gain nothin' by wantin' what someone else has. They always goin' to be someone with more than you and it ain't no good to always be a wantin' all the time. Best be satisfied with what the good Lawd done give and you have a happy life."

That night as Grae rested on a rough blanket on the floor of the slaves' cabin, she thought about Sal's words. She could see how it was good advice for someone who was bound to a life of limits, but she also saw how it applied to her life, her real one. All of the material things in her life that had been taken away when her father went to prison could be wants that would hold her back from being happy. She needed to make the best of what she had now and start from there.

FOURTEEN

The next morning came early. Sal woke Grae up before the sun rose and they had a simple breakfast made as dawn was breaking. She had noticed the night before that a primitive calendar hung on the wall of the cabin with big X's marking off the days. She watched as Bob made an X on Thursday, April 6, 1786. From her grandmother's papers, she knew that in one month, Joseph Baker would be dead.

Grae was sent with Aggie and another Negro named Isaiah to work on planting a vegetable garden. Isaiah was a slave from a neighboring farm. It was a large plot of ground, the biggest garden that Grae had ever seen. She watched as Isaiah took a stake and put it near the far left corner of the ground. He carefully tied twine to it and released the ball of twine as he walked toward her at the other left corner. He put another stake in the ground and tied the twine to it, then he cut the remaining ball away.

"Isaiah, he likes to make the rows straight, says it makes the plants grow better." Grae could tell that Aggie had a soft spot for

Isaiah. Her whole attitude changed with him around. "I just thinks he likes the rows to look nice," she whispered to Grae. Isaiah made several of these staked rows, two feet apart, before Aggie and Grae began planting. They planted seeds all morning and the list of vegetables was longer than Grae would have imagined for that time period. They planted corn, potatoes, several types of beans, peas, turnips, carrots, onions and tomatoes. When they had used the staked rows, they just pulled up the stakes and put them down again two feet from the last one. It was a good system and their planting stayed straight.

"That ground over there that Isaiah be plowing now, we gonna plant that later today. It be all corn. That be for the Massa's whiskey making." Aggie was being friendly to Grae today; she hoped that Isaiah would be around them a lot in the future.

Grae wanted to ask about the whiskey making, but she wasn't so sure she should ask too many questions. It was hard though because she knew that Joseph Baker had been killed while he and Bob and Sam were working in the distillery.

About mid-morning, Aggie left Grae with the planting and went to help Sal finish preparing the noon meal. She knew it was going to be soup beans and corn bread as Sal had begun soaking the dry beans the night before. She'd only been in this new time for twenty-four hours and already she could tell that she had changed. Such a meal was something that years before she would eat at her grandmother's house on a Saturday afternoon visit, with the promise from her mother that they would stop for cheeseburgers on the way home. Now she was ravenous with hunger, and her mouth watered at the thought of the simple meal.

Grae did not know if it was an unusual occurrence, but it looked strange to her to see Mister Baker sitting under a tree eating with Bob. Grae decided to find a place to sit with her meal that was close enough that she might be able to hear part of the conversation. She sat under a smaller tree that was not too far away; sitting with her back to them so that it would not appear as if she was listening.

"We will start a new batch in the barn tonight," Joseph Baker said. "Then we can let it simmer for a few weeks. It will be a good batch if we let it sit until right before the next wagon train comes through. It will bring a high price at the end of the harvest."

Grae did not hear any replies from Bob, but assumed that he was nodding his head or speaking softly. A few weeks of simmering would be just about the time when Joseph Baker was murdered.

"I'd say that those barrels now are ready to bottle." Grae heard the voice of the overseer. She hadn't caught his name yet, but he seemed like a mean sort.

"It's not your business to worry about that none," Joseph Baker replied. "You just see to it that this farm is running right. Bob and I will handle the distillery."

Grae could hear the sound of boots walking toward her. "He got some darkie running his money-making business and me in charge of the hogs." The overseer didn't see Grae behind the tree until he was right on top of her. "What you doing sitting here, girl? Lazy girl, meal time is over, get back to work." Grae jumped up and started walking away. The overseer grabbed her arm from behind, almost jerking it out of the socket. "You keep that pretty little mouth of yours shut, if you know what's good for you. You shouldn't have been eavesdropping on me. I'll make you sorry, if you tell what you heard, and with pleasure." The overseer looked Grae up. "You won't get away from me like you did the wagon master."

Grae squirmed out of his grasp. She could see that Sal was watching from beside the big kettle. She saw hardness in her eyes that must come from a lifetime of seeing evil.

Sal kept her head down and her eyes on the kettle when Grae approached, but that didn't keep her mouth from working just the same. "What he say to you, girl? Tell ole Sal. I know what Missa Mitchell is capable of. He be one mean man."

Grae quickly decided that perhaps she shouldn't tell what the overseer had said or what she had overheard Mister Baker say. "He said I was being lazy sitting there."

"Hmm," Sal said, looking straight at Grae. "Look like he said more than that. You looked like you be scared of him."

Grae put her bean bowl down in the wash pan. "I'm fine. I just need to be quicker about my meal breaks. I don't want to give anyone reason to think I'm lazy."

Sal shook her head. "You just know you can tell ole Sal. Massa Baker he listen to ole Sal, 'cause he know I not be telling no stories." Grae started walking back toward the field to work on planting the corn. As she walked, she could hear Sal start humming and singing.

"The truth shall make us free, Lawd, the truth shall make us free. Oh, my God, one mighty fine day, the truth shall make us free."

"That's it!" Grae said out loud. She looked around cautiously as she put her hand to her mouth. No one was within hearing. "That's why I am here, I'm going to find out the truth."

FIFTEEN

Over the next few days, Grae began to grow accustomed to the early mornings, late evenings and all the work in between. Every day she seemed to learn how to do something and wondered why she hadn't already learned some of these tasks in her real life. A life of privilege was indeed what she had lived and even in an old drafty mansion, her life was a hundred times better than any slave could imagine. She learned that the Bakers were basically good people. Yes, they worked their slaves and other workers from sunrise to sunset, but they were provided for and even allowed to have times of enjoyment.

One of those times was that night, a Saturday. The Baker slaves were allowed to go the Crockett's farm for a gathering. Grae was going to have a rare opportunity, she would be helping Mister Baker and his oldest son, Charlie, work on the whiskey. She was surprised when Mister Baker came to her while she was helping Sal make the breakfast that morning.

"Sal says you are a smart girl and have worked hard this week. Tonight while the slaves are gone, I'm going to find out if you can be trusted. If you can be, you will go with us to the McGavocks in June to their annual summer picnic. All their family comes, so your young man should be in attendance."

Grae hoped that he could not see the less-than-thrilled look that crossed her face. If she had to come face-to-face with the McGavocks, they would soon reveal that she was not engaged to someone in their family. It hit her that it wasn't probably something that she had to worry about anyway. Joseph Baker would not be able to take his family to this event. They would all be in mourning.

Grae stood to the side as the Baker men began their work. She didn't want to appear too eager or too curious, but she was a lot of both. Charlie Baker was very chatty through the process, he reminded her of her freshman year science teacher in the way he phrased his sentences.

"In order to make the best whiskey," Charlie Baker began his description, "you must combine the corn with the water and a sweet substance. This batch includes molasses, but we have, on occasion, used honey or cane sugar."

Grae envisioned a blackboard behind him and could almost see a chemistry formula in chalk. The image almost made her giggle.

"We have to cook it for a couple of weeks over the fire. It is a copper kettle that we use and when the liquid turns to vapor it travels through that coil and condenses." Charlie was pointing now with the end of a big wooden spoon. He really would have made a good science teacher. "Then it goes into this container. We have to strain it and skim it several times throughout the process. Then we store it in oak barrels and that's when it really gets its flavor, the longer it rests, the better it gets." Charlie smiled at his rhyme. Grae could see him doing a whiskey commercial. "Then, we bottle it and sell it."

"Charlie likes to talk," Joseph Baker said from the corner of the barn. Grae had almost forgotten that he was there. "He would have liked to be a teacher, but we need him here." Grae then noticed that Joseph had a bottle in his hand and half of it was gone. Charlie looked away. "Now that you've had your lesson in its making, not that you needed to know that, let's actually see if we can get some work done. Tonight it is time to bottle those two barrels."

Joseph stood up and staggered a bit as he got his balance. He pointed to the barrels again. As she moved closer, she could smell the unmistakable odor of whiskey as its aroma oozed out of the oak wood.

He pointed at Grae. "Not a drop on the ground, not a drop in your mouth. This is how we line our pockets, we need to sell it all." Joseph turned and left, bottle in hand.

"Not a drop on the ground, we must save all the drops for him," Charlie muttered as he moved a box of bottles to the location of the barrel. "I will fill the bottle; you will cork it, and then put it back in the box."

Grae watched as Charlie put the bottle under the tap and began filling it. The liquid was not clear like what she had seen before; this finished brew had a golden brown tint. She imagined that what she had seen in her parent's liquor cabinet had been aged much longer and would have been the expensive kind.

Charlie worked methodically, absorbed in what he was doing, yet somehow far away at the same time. After some time passed, she decided to start a conversation and see if he would reveal any clues into what would later happen.

"You sounded like a teacher there when you told how this whiskey is made." Grae had gotten the hang of inserting the corks, after a few failures. It took a little twisting, but not too much.

Charlie looked directly at her for the first time since they had started working. Grae noticed that Charlie's eyes were so blue that they were almost grey. It was a very unusual color. His hair was mousy brown and curled up on the ends. His stature was small, like his father's; but she could see softness in his facial features that came from his mother.

"Well, I wanted to be a teacher, but Father has other ideas for me." Charlie paused and let out a deep sigh. It was amazing how much a sigh told. "I don't much care for the farm life; I'm just not suited to it. I see beauty in the land and what it produces, but it doesn't stir in my soul to be a part of it."

It was obvious that Charlie had a way with the spoken word; Grae imagined that he might also have talent with the written ones.

"But I am the oldest son; I do not have the luxury of deciding my own fate." Charlie walked past Grae to get another box of bottles. "My father is a good man, as you can see he samples his brew for quality, as all fine Virginia gentlemen do. Distilling is an honorable business. Our own first leader of this New World, Mister Washington, owns the best distillery in our new nation. I believe that I would find myself more suited to the law, like Mister Jefferson."

Grae felt sad for Charlie. If he had been born in her time, it would have been a much easier thing to choose his own path. There were many kinds of slaves in this time period.

"He seems to care for his slaves and workers." Grae noticed a little puddle of whiskey at Charlie's feet under the tap; she got a little bit of straw to absorb it.

"He does, he always has. He's especially fond of Big Bob, but he thinks Sam will eventually cause trouble, he's not the careful sort like Bob."

"I don't believe that Sam has said two words to me." Grae started counting the boxes. Each box had twelve bottles and they had already filled three. "That barrel must hold many bottles."

"It does indeed. We usually yield 150 bottles or more from each barrel. Father was not wrong when he says it lines his pockets."

The evening turned into the night, and Grae and Charlie filled many cases. They had just sat down for a short break when Joseph came wandering back into the barn.

"I should have known that you two would be wasting time." He was stumbling more and had a cigar in his mouth.

"I'd hardly call all those filled cases over there wasting time, Father." Charlie stood up and pointed to the line of boxes along the wall of the barn.

"Well, I guess I misspoke. I just wanted to make sure no one was getting too friendly out here."

Joseph staggered forward and his cigar dropped out of his mouth and into the straw Grae had put under the tap. Instantly it was in flames and Joseph almost staggered into it himself. Charlie grabbed him and pulled him back as Grae took a bucket of water and doused the flames before it reached the barrel.

The incident quickly sobered Joseph up as he looked around and saw what could have happened. The oak barrel was on a wooden table and all the whiskey bottles were in wooden boxes.

"Mister Baker, there was only a few drops of whiskey on the floor, just from where the tap would leak a tad between bottles." Grae knew she had done something risky by speaking to him, but she didn't want Charlie to get into trouble.

"I've bottled plenty of 'shine before, girl, I know what the floor looks like under the tap." Joseph turned and began walking away; his hand was on his head. Charlie looked at Grae and gave her a tiny nod. "You did good with the water," he said without turning around.

After he was out of earshot, Charlie walked back to the tap with a broom and swept up the mess. "That was high praise from Father. I would wager that you will now be moved into the house to help Mother."

Grae thought about that for a moment and wasn't sure if it would help or hurt her from discovering what really transpires when Joseph Baker dies.

"Well, I must do what I am told to do. I don't mind being with the slaves. They have been kind to me."

"Most of them are good natured. Father usually sells the ones who are trouble. Sal and Big Bob came from my mother's family. I think Mother would like for them to be given their freedom, but to stay with us and work for pay."

Grae knew she had now stumbled into a conversation that might really give her some vital information. She must be careful with how she proceeded.

"That is not a practice that happens often, is it? Most people that are born slaves, die slaves, do they not?"

"Yes, in these areas to the South, but I do not think that slavery is as abundant in the North." Charlie began filling up bottles again. "Of course, I think that there is more farming here, perhaps there is more need for slaves."

Grae brought another box of bottles to the tap. "Would you like me to fill the bottles for a while?"

Charlie nodded and sat down to do the corking. "Why are you an indentured servant? You seem very intelligent, as if you came from an educated family."

Grae thought carefully before she answered, making sure that she told the story correctly. "My entire family was planning on coming to America. I have two younger brothers, twins, they are ten years old. About a month before we were scheduled to make the journey, my parents got the typhoid. It took them rather quickly, but neither my brothers nor I took it. As soon as my mother realized what was happening, she sent us to a neighbor's home. We were left with nothing. My brothers were taken to an orphanage. My uncle, he promised to pay my passage to my intended; I knew he owed my father some money, but he signed me into servitude instead."

"I'm very sorry about your parents. If you want, I will post letters for you to your brothers." Charlie was a kind young man. "But why didn't you just find your young man when you arrived, perhaps he could have arranged for your servitude to be suspended?"

Grae paused thinking about what her answer to that might be. "I will not take something that does not belong to me. My freedom doesn't belong to me right now, I must earn it." As she said those words, she thought about her father and what he would have to do to earn his freedom.

Grae was still awake an hour later when the slaves returned from their gathering. They all seemed in good spirits, and Sal chattered on and on about how good the food was and how everyone was dressed. Aggie must have seen Isaiah, because she was humming to herself before she went outside to fetch some water. Even Bob talked to her, asking about how the bottling went. Grae didn't reveal anything about Joseph Baker's condition or the little fire.

"Did Massa Baker help with the bottlin'?"

"No, just me and Charlie."

"Did Massa Baker do some tastin'?" Sal turned and watched Grae. "You can say it, Belle girl; we all knows what goes on."

"Well, some, but not for too long. He stopped."

"Massa, he a good man," Sal sat down next to Grae. "But the whiskey brings out the devil even in a good man."

"There be so many times that he be careless like when he has too much," Bob said. "He stumble around and hurt hisself. I think he got too much pressure on him, too much on his shoulders."

"He be trying to build this farm and make it like farms 'round here," Sal said. "He want to be like the Crocketts and the Sayers, and Lawd help us, the McGavocks." Sal realized the connection. "I don't mean no bad thing, Belle girl, just they got a whole lots and that be hard to catch up to."

Grae nodded her head. This man sitting in front of her could not have murdered his master. This was all sounding stranger. Out of the corner of her eye, Grae noticed something small dart past the open door.

"I need to go to the outhouse."

As she walked through the doorway, she saw the movement again heading toward the barn. She followed; carefully looking around to make sure no one else was within view. As she suspected, it was The General.

"Listen," he said, as they reached the barn. Grae could tell that there were a couple of people in the barn, but didn't know who they were until they started speaking.

"Isaiah say if we could get us a few boxes every few days and hide them. If we could sell them, we would have enough money to run away. You could come with us and haves a new life." It was Aggie talking to Sam. "You know, I could find you a woman." Aggie had her hands on Sam's back, rubbing his shoulders. "Pretty little thing who would know how to take care of you. Maybes we could even get that Belle to goes with us. I sees how you dart your eyes at her."

"She got her a man waiting for her." Sam stood up away from Aggie's hands.

Grae had not seen this coming. She had no idea that Sam was interested in her. This could make her escape difficult.

"You be thinkin' that a McGavock is goin' to marry a servant! She was promised when she was in a fine family, now she like you and me almost. No rich white family gonna welcome that servant girl. Only way she gets a better life now is if she runs." Aggie sounded as if she were in a pulpit preaching a sermon. She was right about one thing, Grae would have to run, right back to her own time, as soon as she found out how to do that.

She started to leave and The General pawed at her ankle. "Listen!"

"I don't care what has to be done, Isaiah done say he's got a wagon hid in the woods far over yonder. All we gots to do is hide some of this 'shine and steal us a horse. We leave one of these nights that Massa gets full of the brew." Aggie seemed to have it all figured out.

"But how you gonna gets Uncle Bob to go along with this? You know he won't do nothing that go against the Massa." Sam was pacing now.

"He not have to know. We say Isaiah over here visitin' me, and he gonna offer to help you so Bob can have an evening with Aunt Sal. We's being nice." Aggie flashed a big smile; she still had all her pearly whites.

"Massa Baker finds out, he will punish Uncle Bob, he will beat him." Sam looked worried.

"Come on now, you think the Massa gonna do anything to Bob. No sir, he thinks Bob is perfect, and he thinks you is trouble. I heard him say it." Aggie walked over and put her arm around Sam. "You don't have no future here, but one of hard labor and short life. You help me and Isaiah, we take you to the Promised Land. We all make a free life together. Bob and Sal and the kids, they be fine, mighty fine. I bets the Missus talks the Massa into given them a plot of land or somethin' one day."

Sam shook his head. "I don't know, sounds like a good way to gets kilt."

"I get you that Belle girl. I make sure she go with us. She be a big help along the way. She could helps us get to freedom. That white skin could lead us to a fine place."

"What I do then?" Sam said.

"You do whats I say." Aggie smiled and a coyote's cry could be heard in a far off field.

Grae took hold of the leather around her neck and inched her fingers down to the key. As she touched it, everything started to sway and go dim.

She awoke to The General licking her face. "What happened to me?"

"You started staggering and then you fell down. Thankfully no one saw you."

"How long have I been out?" Grae sat up and rubbed the back of her neck. She felt hot and strange.

"Just a few minutes, it was probably from exhaustion. I'm sure you didn't work like this in your time."

"And let's not forget that I travelled over 200 years to get here," Grae allowed herself a rare moment of sarcasm; she could use it so infrequently in this world. Life was too hard to be sarcastic about it.

"You better get back to the cabin. If they ask, tell them you were sick." The General started to walk from Grae toward the dark woods. "You heard what they said, now be careful with that knowledge. You can't interfere."

"Why not? I don't want to see Sal and Bob get in trouble."

"Grae, listen to me carefully. One of the rules of time travel is to not change anything."

"But you don't understand. In my time, I learned that Bob and Sam were convicted and hanged for murdering their master, Joseph Baker. I've got to try to stop it."

"No, Grae, you cannot do that. You cannot undo history. If you try, it will change more than just those deaths, it would change lots of people's existence."

"What's the good of travelling in time if you can't fix anything? Why am I even here?"

"Why do you think you are here? What curiosity brought you to this time period?"

"Well, I just didn't think that what little I could find about the murder and conviction made much sense. It just didn't seem to add up to me. I guess I wished that I could know the truth."

"And that is what you will learn then, the truth, what really happened. But just be very mindful, you can't change it. Messing with time can be…"

"Dire and disastrous, I know. It sure will be hard knowing that three people will still die."

"I understand, better than you realize, but trying to change it could cause something worse. Just keep your eyes open and be careful. I'll be watching."

SIXTEEN

Rain fell. The sun shined. Seeds sprouted and grew into healthy plants. All was good on the Baker farm. Just as Charlie had predicted, Grae was moved into the Baker cabin to help Charlie's mother. But she still managed to find a few moments, after the long day of tasks, to go back to the slaves' cabin and continue to teach Sal how to write her name. Actually, Grae taught her to write many things, even a letter to her much older sister who was a slave on a farm in Pennsylvania.

Getting to know the Baker family proved to be more interesting than Grae imagined. While Joseph Baker was usually only in his home from late in the evening until sunrise, Nannie Baker, his wife, was there all the time. Nannie was an average size woman, not petite like Grae's mother, but not large like Sal either. To be only thirty-six years old, she seemed much older. A fact that was perhaps due, in part, to how young she had been when she started living as an adult. Nannie had married in her mid-teens and had all her children before she was 25. This meant that the oldest ones, twins Charles and Rebecca, were already grown and married. Charlie and his wife, Mary, were expecting the first Baker grandchild later that year. They lived in a tiny cabin on the property. Mary spent most of her time during the day with Nannie in the main cabin.

This was a working farm, which Grae learned meant that the slaves mainly did farm work. Sal took care of all the cooking and Aggie did most of the laundry, but inside the main cabin most of the daily tasks were left to Nannie and her children, or now, their new servant.

If Grae had thought cleaning the Mansion was hard, cleaning a cabin in the 1700s was virtually impossible. The cabin had a wood floor, but it seemed as if dirt and dust grew out of the grains of the floorboard. Nannie was obsessed with keeping everything clean, which meant that she wanted Grae to scrub the floors twice a day. With nothing but lye soap, water warmed on the stove, and an ancient brush, it was a tiresome task, but she made the best of it.

Mary was in her early months of pregnancy. She had miscarried the previous year, so she was being extra careful. She would follow Grae from room to room and sit in a chair and watch Grae working, chatting constantly.

"Belle is such a pretty name," Mary said. Grae realized that they were probably about the same age. "I just don't know what name we will give this one."

"It is short for Arabella." Grae watched as a spider crawled across the floor and slid down a hole in the floor. It looked a lot like the one she saw in the closet. She wondered if spiders could travel in time. Not realizing she was smiling, she saw that Mary was still watching her.

"What are you thinking about? Your smile gives you away."

Grae scrambled to think of something to say. "I was remembering a time when I was a girl and me mum took me to see a magician in London."

"It must have been hard losing your parents as you did." Mary looked sad. "I thought I would just cry myself to death when my little one stopped growing and I never got to meet him." Mary twirled a lock of her hair in one hand as the other rested on her growing belly. "What were your parents like?"

Out of the corner of her eye, Grae could see the shadow of Nannie at the doorway listening to their conversation. "Mary, can you sit here on this bed for a few minutes, so that I can move that chair you are in and clean there?"

"Oh, yes, I am so sorry; I shouldn't be in your way."

"You're not in my way at all. I enjoy having your company. It makes the work pass more quickly." From where Grae had moved, she could see Nannie's reflection in the small mirror that hung on the bedroom wall. Nannie was smiling.

"Mary, can you come help me?" Nannie said, making her presence known. "It's about time for the meal, and I need you to set the table."

"Do you need me to help you, Missus Baker?" Grae knew she should always offer to help when tasks were available.

"No, my dear, you are doing a fine job on that floor. I think that Mary can help just fine with this. Sal will be bringing the food soon and Mister Baker and my boys will be eating inside. It's dreadfully hot out there today. Bit of cooling off will help them enjoy their meal."

Grae curtsied and turned to go back to her work. Since she had been moved to work in the main cabin, she had begun curtsying to the Bakers; she thought it would make her appear more British. Perhaps she had watched too many movies.

"You know, Belle, I wasn't sure how we were going to get along. Knowing that you didn't have any servant experience before you came here, I thought it might be hard to get you to work, but you are a very good worker."

"Thank you, ma'am, that would make my dear mum beam with pride it would. I am no stranger to work. My brothers and I all had chores to do, at home and at the store."

"The store, you say, your parents had a store?" Nannie seemed very interested in this last tidbit of information.

"The store belonged to my father and my uncle. It had been their father's and his before him. It was a mercantile."

"Why aren't you there then, helping your uncle?"

"My uncle is not a kind man. He didn't want to help me and my brothers when my parents passed. He just wanted to be rid of us. He could put the boys in an orphanage, but he shipped me away."

"Belle, now you tell me the truth. Were you sent here to marry?" Nannie held out her arms for Grae to come to her. "You tell me, there will be no trouble for the truth."

Grae allowed Nannie to envelope her in a hug. It felt good to have this comfort. "No ma'am, I was not. My uncle just signed me into servitude. He gave me a choice. I could stay there and be a servant or come to the New World. I thought that maybe I could come here and build a wonderful new life, and then send for my brothers later. I have no one here waiting for me."

"Why did you lie?"

"Why does anyone lie?" Grae walked toward the small window. "It sounds better than the truth."

"So you don't know the McGavocks?"

Grae paused before answering. "Not in this life."

SEVENTEEN

Some evenings after the day's work was done, Charlie would have Grae help with the whiskey making. It seemed that they were doing a lot of bottling and accumulating many cases of whiskey. This particular evening, Grae was given the task of putting straw and wood shavings between the bottles in the boxes. This brew was no doubt destined for saloons in the West and bars in the North; Southerners had plenty of their own.

"Massa Charlie, when does you think the wagon master gonna come again?" It was one of the few times Grae heard Sam speak. Since overhearing the conversation between Aggie and Sam, Grae was careful around them both. Aggie had already started telling Grae she would never be accepted into any good family. She knew it wouldn't be long before she would begin asking her to run away with them.

"Well, Sam, I'm not sure, seems like for a while there was a wagon master through here every few weeks, but we haven't seen one in almost two months now."

"It's gonna take several of them to haul all this whiskey."

"That not be any of your concern, Sam, that be the Massa's business," Bob spoke up and Grae could see that he was giving Sam a stern look.

Sam kept right on talking. "Massa Charlie, I be thinkin' that you might needs some extra help the night that the Sayers has their big ole wedding party. You and the Missus gonna be going to that, ain't you?"

"Well, we may do that. It all depends on how Mary is feeling then."

"I was just thinkin' that Isaiah from over at the Sayers farm, he be a good worker and maybe he could help for a little wages. You see, his mammy, she done be up North somewheres and needin' some care."

"Samuel, don't you be makin' such notions to Massa Charlie. He knows how to gets extra help." Grae could see Bob's jaw clinching in anger, but Sam wasn't paying any attention. Grae knew why he was so determined and it scared her a little.

"No, Bob, Sam has a good idea and I will pass it on to Father. We may need some help that night." Charlie turned to Grae. "You can go now. Mother will be wondering why I have kept you so long."

Grae bowed her head and turned to walk away. She could feel Sam's eyes on her and she wasn't quite sure what she could do to make him feel differently.

Late that night when all the Bakers were sound asleep, Grae began to cry. She felt as if she had been away from her family for years. The General told her that no time would pass at home during her journey, but it sure didn't make these days any easier. All these weeks, she tried to stay focused on why she was there and think of it as a dream from which she would soon awaken. But on nights like this, when tiredness did not welcome sleep, she couldn't hold back any longer. From childhood, she'd always gotten the hiccups when she cried and now she found herself lying in a bed in 1786 sobbing and hiccupping. She tried to be quiet, but hiccups are hard to hide, so she got up and crept out to the front room. She would very quietly go outside and get some water. She was just about to reach for the doorknob when a voice startled her.

"They are hard to get over. My mother used to make me swallow a spoonful of sugar." The voice belonged to Joseph Baker. He was sitting in his chair next to the fireplace. The light of the new moon coming through the window made him appear like a ghost sitting there. As her eyes adjusted and her nose began to wake up, she realized that he was also smoking a pipe, the fog around his head contributed to the ominous look.

"I'm very sorry to disturb you, sir; I didn't think anyone was (hiccup) up."

"I am up and down throughout most nights. Don't know what causes it, but my legs twitch when I lay down. So I get up and sit in this chair and sip this elixir." Joseph Baker picked up the bottle. "I know it will be the death of me."

Grae was stunned and mesmerized by the words. In fact, it shook the hiccups right out of her. "I think I am better now, sir. I shall bid you good night and return to bed."

"Yes. I hear good things of you. Perhaps I shall allow your servitude to be shortened. I know you have spent many extra hours helping Charlie with the distilling, and Sal tells me you have taught her to write a letter."

"I hope this does not displease you. I meant no harm. She wanted me to write a letter to her elder sister, and I thought it would be good practice."

"No, no, don't be alarmed." Joseph Baker shook the bottle as he talked, some of the liquid sloshed onto his trousers. "You can teach Sal whatever she can learn. My wife will be pleased. I want only good for Sal and Bob. Sam and Aggie, well, I'm not so sure they are as good Negroes as their aunt and uncle, but I cannot complain about the level of work, at least when I am there to see it."

Grae turned and went back to the room where her small bed stood waiting. She looked back over her shoulder. She could still see the small puffs of smoke that were gently lighted by the moon. Joseph Baker only had a few more days of life. Despite his human faults, he was a good man; she wished she could help him survive what lay before him. As she climbed into her bed, she thought of her own father. He was no doubt sitting in a prison cell on a bed not much better than what she was now on. "I know you don't believe me, but not all of this is true." Those were the words he said to her on their last visit before his official sentence began. She wondered if she would ever know the whole truth in her own time.

EIGHTEEN

May opened its arms wide and declared that summer had come early. Purple phlox, wild mustard, and iris were blooming everywhere. The fields were alive with growing plants and talk of an early harvest was frequently spoken. Several weeks had passed since Grae landed in this time. Occasionally she would catch glimpses of The General and surmised that she was always under his watchful eye.

Her life as Belle was quite firm by then. Since she revealed that there was no suitor waiting, Nannie had very obviously decided to try and find her a real one. In the hushed tones of the night, Grae overhead conversations between Nannie and her husband about what "good young men" in neighboring farms might be suitable. Joseph admonished his wife that he wasn't sure that those families would be too thrilled to have their son marry a servant girl. Nannie insisted that they need not know.

"Where but for the grace of God go our children, Joseph? We are not here on this land so long that we cannot see our own families living across the water. Losing her parents and having her brothers taken away, while that heartless uncle sold her, she needs someone to show a kind eye her way."

"And I suppose that someone would be you, my wife?" Grae could hear a chuckle in Joseph's voice, a clear sound of love. He had not brought a bottle in that night. "So who shall you pass her off to be at the Sayers' wedding party? I know that's when you are thinking of working your matchmaking charms."

"I cannot hide from you, can I?" Grae heard a young giggle in Nannie's voice as well and instantly felt embarrassed that she was listening to this private conversation. "I think we shall say that she was sent to live with us, for that is not a lie, by some distant family. Who knows, we could be related to the lass."

"And have you already made her a dress for Saturday?" Joseph seemed to now be enjoying this conversation.

"Mary has found one of her good dresses from before she married Charlie and tomorrow we are going to have Belle try it on and see what alterations need to be made. Belle is close to the size that Mary was when she married, I think it will do just fine."

"The young man then, have you chosen him also? For he does not stand a chance if both you and Mary are in on the scheme."

Grae heard the sound of a boot falling to the floor, followed by its mate.

"You think you are the sly one. You think we have it all planned out. We shall let nature take its course." The rustle of sheets and quilts moving told Grae that the Bakers were now in bed for the night. "But if a young McGavock took a fancy to her, I wouldn't be disappointed." The last sound Grae heard was a hearty laugh from Joseph.

"I already have a McGavock," Grae said softly to herself, "if I can only find my way home to him."

"I told you that I would work on Belle and I'm doin' it." Grae stopped short of turning the corner to the back of the slave cabin when she heard Aggie talking. "It will all be fine. Come Sunday mornin', we be on our way to New York."

"I don't believe you!" Sam replied, there was a strong tone of anger in his voice. "I hears Massa Charlie talkin' to Miss Mary about her and Missus Baker makin' Belle a dress for the party at the Sayers'. Says they gonna have her married off in no time. You lied to me!"

Grae quickly moved behind a tree where she could see what was happening. Aggie had a big basket full of clothes in her hands. Sam was holding an ax. It appeared that he had been chopping wood and stacking it beside the barn where the whiskey was made. Now he was slinging that ax around in anger.

"No, no, no such thing, Sam." Aggie put the basket down and walked toward him with her hands out as if she was trying to calm him. "Aggie wouldn't lie to her Sam. We has been together since we was babies, we has. I gonna fix it, I fix it right up."

"You can't fix what the Massa and his missus done want. You can't fix nothin'. It been decided. Here I done help you and Isaiah, I took at least a dozen boxes of 'shine out of that barn." Sam started backing Aggie up against the back of the cabin. She almost fell walking backwards trying to get away. "You know what the Massa do to me if I were caught?" Sam was holding the ax, his right hand up near the head, and his left on the other end. "You know what he do?"

Aggie looked very scared and Grae started to come out from her hiding place. She felt something up against her leg and looked down to see The General.

"Don't move," he said.

"This is what the Massa would do." Sam took the handle and broke it in two with his bare hands. Snapping it like it was a twig. Sam threw the two pieces down on the ground. Aggie was still trembling and slowly fell down to the ground. "I gets you the whiskey. But you won't get me what I want. It's done gone."

"We've got to make sure that you are safely at that party on Saturday night. You know what the date is."

Grae thought about what The General had just said. "It will be May 6. That's the day that…"

"Yes, and you need to be safely somewhere else."

Grae paused and looked back at Sam and Aggie. He had picked up the pieces of the ax and was already making a new handle to go on it. Aggie had gotten up and retrieved the basket of laundry and was walking toward the main cabin. It was like watching people in slow motion.

"No, I think you are wrong about that. I think I need to be there when it happens. It's the only way that I will know the truth."

"Grae, listen to me. You will be stuck in this time if you try to stop it. You will never see your family again."

"I didn't say anything about stopping it."

"Grae, it will be a bloody mess, but you can't prevent it. It will always be in your memory. You take the memories you make here with you."

"I know I can't prevent it, but I want to know the real story. I want to know why three men die. Maybe the truth will make a difference in my time.'

"Oh, Grae, stop being naïve, you will not be able to tell anyone. What good will it be for you to know?"

"I'll have to figure that out."

"Just make sure that you don't do anything that makes Sam want to treat you like he did that ax handle. There's a rage behind that strength and someone will get hurt."

In between the standard chores, Nannie and Mary found time to work on the dress for Grae to wear on Saturday. While the dress would hardly fit on a fashion runaway in the 21st century,

Grae thought that it may have been one of the most beautiful pieces of clothing she had ever seen.

"My mother loved to wear bright clothes," Mary said as she worked on pinning the hem of the dress. Mary was about two inches taller than Grae. "My father thought that it was sinful to wear anything that had red in it, but my mother argued him down. 'Why, Abner, there are pretty red poppies out in that field that the Lord created. Why would he make a flower that color if it was sinful?'"

The fabric was soft cotton. The background was an unusual shade of pink that leaned toward a light red. White flower motif designs softened the color and red and blue/green flowers seemed to jump off from every angle. The flowers were carnations and daisies in several sizes. The design of the dress fit at the waist with a square neck in front and back, and puffy sleeves. From the waist, it flowed delicately to the floor and there were tiny bows at several points that pulled the fabric up from the floor and a larger bow in the back. Grae thought it was beautiful.

As Grae stood awestruck looking at herself in the mirror, Nannie came up behind her. "I suppose you must have had nicer fabric than this in your family's store. It's hard for us to get much fabric out here."

"I don't think I have ever seen anything more beautiful."

Mary stood up and hugged Grae from behind. "This was the dress I wore the day that Charlie asked me to marry him."

"Oh, it's so special then, you shouldn't change it for me. You might want to give it to one of your daughters."

"No, it will be special for you. They will have their own special dresses. If we had time and the material, we would make one just for you."

Grae turned back to the mirror. "Oh, I think it's wonderful. I wish I could wear it to the prom."

"What did you say?" Nannie asked.

Grae realized she had made a big slip. "I said, I wish I could wear it prominently to every special occasion." She knew that sounded lame, but hoped it made a little sense.

"Well, the thing about dresses is that you don't get new ones very often," Nannie said, "so you probably will be wearing it many times in the future."

Grae breathed a big sigh of relief. It had been hard to edit every sentence that she spoke and make it "future-free," but a slip up could lead to questions, ones she couldn't afford to answer.

Later that evening, Grae went to the slaves' cabin to help Sal write another letter. She was careful to choose a time when she didn't think that Sam was around. He was in the barn helping Charlie. As she entered the cabin, she found Bob telling Sal about something that had happened that morning. "I was walkin' through the north field and I looked up to where that old hickory tree stands tall and stout and I sees myself sittin' under it."

"What are you sayin'? That heat done got to you early in the day." Sal shook her head and continued to stir something in a pot on a small stove.

"No, woman, it was the cool of the mornin'. I rubs my eyes and look again and theres I sit under the tree, but I ain't movin'. Someone be sittin' on the other side of the tree behinds me, but I can't see who it be." Sal had now sat down at the table across from Bob. "And thens what I seen really scares me. I sees you and the young'uns, you be standin' below and you are cryin' and wailin' and I can't gets to you."

Sal stood up and walked back to the stove. She darted her eyes at Grae, but didn't say anything.

"You think it's a sign, don't you, Sal? Lawd, have mercy, what more can this family stand before it crumbles to pieces? We was born into slavery and there we shall die, but the years in between are filled with pain beyond the labor."

Grae sat there thinking that she had heard about something like this before. Someone seeing himself dead before it happened. She would have to think about where she heard it.

"Now, Bob, don't be goin' on silly like that. You just tired is all. This is an extra hard time of year. Has that Sam been pullin' his weight? He be lazy sometimes. He old enough now to work like a man."

"He workin' all right, but his mind be somewheres else. Probably thinkin' about some girl." Bob looked around. "Where be Aggie?"

"She still outside workin' the laundry. She get behind somehow. Girl's head always in them clouds."

"I thinks that Isaiah be trouble. I hears the Massa say that Missa Sayers gonna sell him next time wagon master come through. He be stealin'. Aggie need to stay away from him or she be sent away too, or worse."

"Lawd, I guess I be talkin' to her then. Stubborn like her mama, it be hard to get her to hear different. She got big eyes for that man."

"Massa says that you and me cans go to the wedding party on Saturday and helps Missa Sayers workers. Says there be some mighty good food and we cans hear the music. I be worried about the whiskey makin' though."

"Don't make no difference to me. I just as soon stay here and rest my tired body as to go over yonder to watch some poor folk act fancy." Sal remembered that Grae was in the room. "But I hears there be a girl who be having a pretty new dress for the party. I hears Miss Nannie say that Massa Baker gonna cut down her time and let her go marry if the time be right."

Grae shook her head in embarrassment. "I feel strange about all of that. Miss Mary shouldn't be giving me her dress and I should work out my time."

"Honey girl, don't you dare say that!" Sal shouted. The sound was so powerful that it scared her. "Someone gonna be nice to you, you let them. In this world, there is plenty of evil and hate. When you see good comin' your way, you run up to meet it."

As much as Grae wanted to go home, she knew deep in her heart that she would miss Sal. She had learned a lot from this woman. She was owned by another human being, but she still had the decency in her heart to want to do what was right by them and all those around her. Sal would no doubt die a slave and have very few possessions of her own in her entire years on this Earth; but she was richer than many of the people Grae knew in her time. This was someone who Grae would carry with her for the rest of her life.

"You know, Sal, just in case I don't get to say this later. I love you and I appreciate all you have done for me."

Sal opened up her arms for a wide hug. It was a feeling that Grae wanted to never forget.

"Belle girl, you have been like sunshine on a dark day. I be glad God sent you to this farm." After a long hug, Sal started hollering. "Lawd have mercy, I've done burned this bread for sure."

The moment was gone, but Grae wouldn't forget it.

NINETEEN

"You should have seen the look on Sal's face, she was scared." On the afternoon of the next day, Grae had a rare few moments with The General. She told him what Bob said about seeing himself sitting under the tree. She had been sent by Nannie to pick red raspberries for several pies that Sal would be making for Saturday. With the unusually early summer-like weather, everything was coming in early. "I know I have heard that somewhere before, I just can't remember where."

"It's Doppelganger. It's seeing yourself, like a double. It's supposed to foretell evil or misfortune."

"I don't know that I have ever heard that word, but I've heard some famous story about it." Grae was eating more raspberries than she was putting in her pail. "These are so sweet. It's like they are magic. Do you want some?"

"Really, Grae, do you think that cats eat raspberries?"

"I'm sorry, sometimes I forget that you are a cat. Well, you really aren't a cat inside, are you? Who are you really?"

"That subject is for another day." The General turned his back with his tail in the air and began to pace like a college professor in a classroom. "I would imagine that the story you are trying to remember is about Abraham Lincoln, an esteemed President, who in reference to the current time we are living in, has not been born yet."

"Wow, that's hard to imagine. He's one of the old Presidents."

"As I was saying, on the evening of his first election as President, he was tired after the activities of the day and he reclined on a sofa to rest. He looked across the room and saw his own image, full length, in a mirror; but he had two faces. This disturbed him, so he got up and walked toward the mirror, but the image disappeared. He laid back down and looked again and the image reappeared. He then noticed that one of the two faces was several shades paler than the other. A few days later, still haunted by the sight, he told his wife about it. She said that it was a sign that he would be elected to a second term, but would not live to complete it."

"Oh my, yes, that is what I remembered. I did a report on Mister Lincoln in my freshman year and read several of his biographies. That's a rather ominous story, and we know that it will be true for Bob as well." Grae had stopped picking berries while The General told the story. "I guess I better finish picking before someone starts looking for me."

The General followed behind her as she continued. The sun had grown hot, but off in the distance the Blue Ridge Mountains hid the rumblings of a storm to cool the day and quench the thirst of the fields. "I am amazed at how you have handled this journey. I've not seen you act like a teenager of your time. You've shown great maturity and you've worked hard here. Your mother would be proud."

"You've mentioned my mother several times. Do you know her somehow?"

The General began to walk away from Grae, off into a field. "Our paths crossed for a time, it was long ago."

"If you tell me who you are, I can tell her that I met you."

"You need to concentrate on returning to your time. Don't be concerned about me. I have been here for a very long time."

"But…" Grae stopped, again he had vanished. It seemed as though he could tell when she needed to talk to him; but was only willing to divulge just so much.

Friday came and with it much activity on the Baker farm. Because of the wedding events at the Sayers' the following day, extra work had to be done. It seemed as if everyone from slave to master was busy with many different tasks. After dinner was consumed, Grae found herself helping Aggie wash a mountain of dishes. She tried not think about the true cleanliness of the dishes. Her mother's obsession with cleaning had found its way into her genes, but she realized that she lived in a different time and had to accept what was deemed acceptable.

"I don't understand why you be goin' to that Sayers' party tomorrow. You thinks there be some fine young white man there who is gonna take a fancy to you. None of them gonna want a servant girl. You should find youself a hardworkin' man like Sam and be satisfied with your place."

Grae did not respond to Aggie. She knew there was no sense in arguing. Aggie had a plan for her own happiness and what Grae thought did not matter.

"I heard that there ain't no McGavock waitin' for you. That was just a lie."

"It doesn't matter. I was honest about the lie."

"Now all those fine white folk gonna know that you are a liar. They won't want their sons marryin' a liar."

"Missus Baker will not tell them that."

"She might not, but ole Aggie sure will."

"Why would you do that?" Grae heard herself ask the question and shook her head. Why was she letting Aggie pull her into this conversation?

"I knows where your place is and it is with us."

"You can't decide my place. I decide my place!" Maybe it was the weeks of laborious work or maybe it was her shear frustration at being away from her own world; but all of a sudden a mountain of frustration was building inside of Grae.

"You get off your high horse. You just be a white slave and you got no business thinkin' you gonna be somebody!"

"I am going to that party and I am going to be somebody!" Grae turned to leave. She didn't even know what she was saying anymore. She was ready for this to be over.

"I'll fix it so you don't want to be seen at no party." Before Grae could turn and respond, Aggie took hold of the braid that held her long black hair. She tried to pull free, but instead heard the cutting sound of her hair being sliced off and its weight leaving her body. She jerked so fast that she felt the tip of Aggie's knife cut into the back of her neck. She tumbled and everything went black.

She woke up in her bed in the Baker cabin with Nannie and Sal hovering around her.

"She open them eyes. You says something to ole Sal now, Belle girl."

They both looked worried. Joseph Baker stood at the door. He just looked mad.

"Can you speak to us, Belle? Are you hurting anywhere? You took a hard fall after you cut yourself." Nannie looked pale. Grae noticed that Mary was also in the room, sitting in the corner, holding her stomach.

"Cut myself? What are you talking about?" Grae saw Aggie come into view. She had been standing behind Sal.

"I told them that you just all of a sudden started actin' crazy. That you was hollerin' and carryin' on about your dead mama and that you took one of the knives we was washin' and started jabbin' in the air like you was after somethin'."

Grae looked hard and deep into Aggie's eyes. She wasn't sure if what she saw was fear, anger, or plain crazy; but she didn't want to cross that line with her, whichever it was.

"I don't remember that." Grae thought that was a safe response. It seemed to appease Aggie. She shook her head and there was a glimmer of satisfaction on her face.

"I not be surprised. I was afraid you had the fever or somethin' the ways you be actin'." Realizing that she had an audience, Aggie started pouring on the drama. "Then she said somethin' about havin' the Devil's hair and she retched round and grabbed ahold of her hair and with the other hand she took that knife and cut it off with one slice." Aggie demonstrated what she was saying. Grae rolled her eyes. Sal saw this and knelt down next to her.

"You not faintin' again, is you? Aggie, make youself useful and hand me that pan of water." Aggie did as Sal asked, but kept telling her story.

"I be tryin' to get that knife out of her hand for she kilt herself and the point it went down into her neck. I pried it outs of her hand as she fell to the ground. It be like she was possessed."

Grae couldn't take any more and sat straight up in the bed. The sudden movement made her dizzy. It was then that she realized she had hit her head as it now felt like it weighed a hundred pounds. She fell back into Sal's arms, as the woman caught her.

TWENTY

The next day was Saturday, May 6, 1786. The sun rose bright that morning, but Grae was already awake. Sleep had been restless. Her head hurt, her body ached, and her heart, it cried for what was and what would be. As she slowly sat up in bed, her bandaged hand went back to the nape of her neck. No longer did her long black hair cascade down her back. She knew without looking at it that its signature unusual color was fading. If she was able to return to her time, she would return changed, that surely broke some level of rule.

Aggie's lies saved the slave from certain brutal punishment, but it cast doubt on Grae's sanity and that was like the Devil's curse. This young country had already hanged women in the northern colonies for being accused of witchcraft, insanity would, in primitive terms, be just as bad. Grae needed someone to believe that she was okay without invoking the wrath of Aggie. She learned the previous night that Aggie would stop at nothing to get what she wanted, even if that meant harming Grae.

Grae went to the basin and splashed water on her face. She could tell by the noise she heard in the adjoining room that the Baker family was already up and busy with the day. Allowing her to rest and recover was a kindness or a caution on their part, and she would soon discover which one. The discovery would seal her fate. Looking out the small window, she saw tall trees, their green branches reaching to a hopeful sky. Buzzards circled overhead, there was something dead below.

"Not yet, old birds, but the time is coming. Death shall come before tomorrow's dawn."

"Belle, I heard you stirring in here. How are you feeling?"

Grae turned to see Nannie standing before her. She was wiping her hands on a dull white apron that hung around her middle. Grae stared at her a moment, she wanted to remember her. It was clear that she had been a beauty; a soft grace was hiding under lines of a too-hard pioneer life. Grae could see her living in a modern day with less hard work and harsh sun, more simple luxuries and good makeup. She could see her mother in that face, mid-thirties shouldn't look so tired.

A sick feeling came upon Grae as she realized that this would probably be the worst day of Nannie's life. There would be good and bad throughout the rest of her days, but this would be the one, the single day, that at the end of her life she would deem to have the most misery, the most long-lasting grief. Grae wished for the power to change the course of time, but knew even without The General's warning that to meddle would be dire and disastrous indeed.

"I feel a little sore," Grae said quietly and calmly as her hand again went to the back of her neck.

"Your beautiful hair, your shining glory," Nannie ran her hand over the now-short strands, "you didn't do this to yourself." Grae's eyes grew big and searched Nannie's face. "You need not answer. We know. Joseph and Sal and I, we know that you did not do this. I have known you only for a short time, but I have known Aggie all her life. These are her actions, not yours."

"I just don't know…She scared me."

"You are right to be scared. There is much anger in her heart. It is not all her fault. Like many in her place, she wants things this world will not allow her." Nannie drew Grae into her arms. "I look at you and I see my own daughters. This is why I do not want you in servitude. You will always be in danger when someone owns you."

Grae thought these words ironic from someone who was an owner herself. But perhaps that was who had the best understanding of the arrangement. She doubted that it came natural for one human to own another.

"We know we must do something about Aggie. It will break Sal's heart, but she knows as well." Nannie turned to walk back into the main room. "There is much to do this morning. We must be at the Sayers' by half past two."

"I'm still going?"

"Well, of course you are." Nannie watched as Grae reached for her hair. "Mary and I have been thinking about your hair and we think we have a way to hide its shortness. You have such a pretty frock to wear, no one will notice your hair. Leave it to us."

As much as she appreciated this kindness, she needed to be in the barn that night. She needed to know what really happened.

Sal and Nannie spent the morning making pies. They made ones with the red raspberries Grae had picked, as well as, apples with the wonderful smell of cinnamon.

True to her word, Nannie and Mary fixed her hair to hide its shortcomings. Mary had fashioned a bow out of some of the extra material that came off of the hem of the dress. They attached it to a piece of ribbon and pinned Grae's hair back. Sal took a long round piece of iron that almost looked like a candle, she stuck it in the fire for a few moments and then wrapped a group of strands around it near Grae's face. After a few moments, she unwound it and there was a perfect ringlet in its place. She did this several times around Grae's face. It was beautiful.

"How in the world did you imagine how to fix my hair so perfectly?" Grae looked in the small mirror in amazement. "I can't even tell that my hair is so short, it looks like it is pinned up in a bun. The bow hides it."

Nannie looked at Sal and they both released a hearty laugh. "Mary shall enjoy this story. When Charlie and Rebecca were little, they were always fighting. I had other small children as well and they ended up on their own quite often." Nannie looked out the window. "I had been working on making a shirt for Joseph and had my cloth and needles and scissors lying about. I didn't think they were within their reach. I went outside to get a bucket of water and when I came back Charlie and Rebecca were sitting in the floor. Charlie had cut Rebecca's hair. It was almost as short as yours. I will never forget the look on Joseph's face. He said, 'Well, I thought we had a boy and a girl, but it looks like we have twin boys now.' We still laugh about that sometimes."

Everyone grew silent, allowing Nannie her time in thought. There was a stillness to the air, like before a thunderstorm arrives. There would be no storms today. There was not a cloud in the sky. But there was something coming. It hummed in the distance.

Grae didn't know that you could fit so many people on one wagon. It was loaded tight with people. Behind it was a small wagon, driven by Bob, with Sal in the back, and all the pies. Grae had not seen Aggie all morning. No one had mentioned her name but Nannie. It was decided that in the early evening, Bob and Charlie would return to work on the whiskey. Mister Baker had heard a report that the wagon master was stopped for a couple of days in Draper's Meadow. He might arrive as early as Monday.

This wagon master had multiple wagons in his transport. He might buy the Baker's whole stock of whiskey.

Grae thought she looked like an old-fashioned doll. In her fitted dress and hair pulled back, she wished someone could take a photo and email it to her. But she was two hundred years too early for that. So she carefully sat down in the back of the Baker's wagon and tried not to wrinkle her dress. It was a bumpy ride over hills and once through a wooded section. The view was beautiful. Grae realized that she hadn't slowed down enough since moving to Virginia to enjoy the mountains. It was easy to see why so many people had travelled through the area and decided to stop, whether for a few days or for generations. The colors of the landscape were beautiful, and they seemed to melt into one another. It was like a painting in which the artist's stroke gave a colorful movement to all that was in view.

Grae knew she was near the Sayers' farm from the sound rather than view. The horses climbed up and crested a hill as the sound of the music met them. As the farm became visible, Grae realized why Joseph Baker worked so hard. He wanted to build a plantation life for his children and grandchildren and a farm like this was what he was reaching for.

After they all climbed out and the wagon was pulled away, Mary took Grae by the hand and introduced her to some of the young women who were there. She could tell that this was a duty bestowed on her by Nannie, an effort to begin Grae's introduction into this community, not as a servant, but just as a young woman. Grae smiled and nodded and tried to appear interested, but what she really wanted to do was explore the property. So when the talk turned to babies and all the attention reverted to Mary, Grae slipped away.

The wedding ceremony had occurred in a small church nearby that morning. This event was a gathering for the bride and groom, a celebration. Several long tables for eating had been constructed in the field with almost as many laid out with food. The children had numerous games underway with laughter filling the air. The men were either pitching horseshoes or telling tall tales. The women were buzzing like bees preparing the food tables or whispering to each other about this or that.

There were four barns of various sizes within view of the main house. This was not a cabin, but a two-story structure, built of stone and wood. It appeared to have at least four or more rooms on each floor. Grae hoped that she would be invited inside. She would love to see if it resembled the older portion of the Mansion.

The only cabins on the property appeared to be slaves' quarters or work areas. She peeked into several and found a smokehouse with hams hanging from the rafters, a springhouse that was cool for the weather, and several that looked as if they were for storage. She felt like she was spying, a fact that was confirmed when she turned around from looking inside one and found herself facing the buttons on someone's vest. She let out a small scream and almost fell back through the doorway.

"My apologies, I didn't mean to startle you." Grae followed the voice up the chest of buttons to the face that it was coming from. She gasped again as she recognized it.

"What are you doing here?" Grae looked around behind him. "How did you get here?"

"Well, I rode here on my horse. I was supposed to have come on the wagon with my family, but I thought it was a beautiful day for a ride."

"What? You couldn't possibly have…" Grae looked more closely at the person before her. The blond hair, the blue eyes, the physique, the young man standing before Grae was the spitting image of Gav. He smiled and a tear ran down her face.

"I didn't mean to make you cry. I'm so sorry, I will leave you." He made a little bow and turned to go.

"No, stop! I'm not crying." Grae quickly smeared away the tear. "It's my allergies."

"Your what?" The young man looked puzzled.

"Ah, well, that's what we call it in England. When…" Grae was having a hard time fixing this one. She looked up and squinted. "When you look at the sun and it hurts your eyes."

"Oh, well, I've never heard that. Then, let's go find some shade and let your beautiful eyes rest a spell." The young man motioned for Grae to walk away from the cabins and to a small grove of large trees nearby.

"I do not believe that I caught your name." Grae was not sure how to properly introduce herself in this situation.

"My apologies, how unchivalrious of me. My name is James Patrick McGavock. I am called Patrick."

"Very nice to make your acquaintance, Patrick. My name is Gr…Arabella Young. Most people call me Belle."

"Grarabella. That's an unusual name." Patrick smiled as if he knew that it had been a mistake.

"You must have misheard me. My name is Arabella. Is it my accent that keeps confusing you?" Grae hoped her sarcastic tone was not lost in this time period.

"I see, well, Miss Young, will you be staying at the Baker farm long?"

"How did you know?"

"I saw you arrive with them. I presumed you were their guest, a relative perhaps?" Grae was not sure if this was a genuine courtesy question or a trick one. Perhaps Patrick already knew her place with the Bakers.

"I am not sure how long I will be staying, but while I am there I am in their service."

"Very well." Patrick turned and looked toward the activities below them near the house. "It looks like the dancing has started. Shall we join them?"

"It does not bother you that I am a servant in the Bakers' home?"

"I do not wish servitude on any person. But in my humble opinion, it is far worse to be ashamed of your position in life than the position itself. You have given me a straightforward and honest answer, without apology for it. That tells me a great deal about your character and virtues." Patrick looked directly into Grae's eyes. "And you have very beautiful and unusual eyes."

Grae smiled. This was Gav reincarnated. Or perhaps Gav was Patrick. It was nice to be in the presence of a friend.

Throughout the rest of the afternoon, Grae danced quite frequently with Patrick. When other young men came forward and asked for a dance, Patrick told them that she was tired from dancing and pointed them to other young ladies. Just like his athletic parallel in the 21st century, Patrick was great at blocking and interceptions.

The wedding meal was very impressive, even to a girl whose mother hosted many fancy garden parties. There was a huge pig cooked over a fire on a spit and wild turkeys had been roasted. One long table was full of all sorts of side dishes, mostly vegetables of the season. While the recipe for mayonnaise had been created by this time, it had not become a household staple, so the traditional assortment of summer salads that Grae was used to were not on the festive table. The dessert table, however, looked a little more familiar with pies and cakes of many flavors.

As the sun began to set, Nannie approached Grae as she was sitting on a bench with Patrick. He rose and bowed. "Good evening, Missus Baker."

"Good evening, Patrick, I see you have made our Belle's acquaintance." Nannie winked at Grae.

"I have indeed, ma'am, our conversation has been delightful. Her young life has been filled with adventure."

Grae giggled at the last comment.

"Belle, Joseph and I are going to return to the farm with Bob. Joseph is concerned about the work in the barn. We will ask Charlie to accompany us."

"Oh, I would be glad to go in Charlie's place. You know that I am capable of helping with the work." Grae was so caught up in her time with Patrick that she'd forgotten what was going to transpire that night. "I do not mind. Wouldn't it be lovely for Charlie to have this evening with Mary? He works so hard. They will soon be busy with their own family. Let me work in his place. I owe this to all of you."

"Missus Baker, if I may be so bold to say, I would love to have the opportunity to train under your husband. My father has told me that Mister Baker's distillery skills are excellent. I would be glad to accompany him this evening and see if I could be of some assistance."

Nannie smiled and nudged Grae. "I'm sure that he would love to have you as an apprentice." She thought for a moment. "That is very kind of you, Grae. With the two of you going, perhaps I shall stay here and assist Missus Sayers with the evening's activities. Ardelia has been such a good friend to me through the years. I shall go and speak to Joseph. Meet me at the wagon."

"So, do all young gentlemen need to learn the art of whiskey making?" Grae asked.

"Why, our own first President, Mister Washington, is said to have the largest and most successful distillery in our new nation, and Mister Jefferson is an expert at winemaking. It would seem that making these libations are very reputable trades."

"Well, it would surely be more beneficial for you to see the process from the beginning. Tonight's work is more the task of completion."

"You seem to be fluent in the process." Patrick looked at her questioningly.

"I have been assisting Charlie since I arrived here. I have learned a great deal."

"Miss Arabella Young, I do think you are a young woman ahead of your time. You are someone I shall not forget."

"Mister Patrick McGavock, I am a young woman out of my time, and I am certain that I shall never forget you." Grae realized she had experienced something unique and rare. She had truly known someone in two different times. Gav would not know it, but perhaps it explained why he had been drawn to the new girl who lived in SpookyWorld.

Grae and Patrick were waiting at the wagon with Bob when Joseph and Nannie approached. It was the edge of dark, but Joseph appeared to have a half empty bottle of his own whiskey in his hand. He had brought a case to Mister Sayers for the event. Joseph seemed to have trouble with his footing and stumbled once as they watched him approach. Grae saw what would be a catalyst for the night ahead.

"Where's Charlie?" Joseph said, as he got near the wagon.

"Belle is going to work in his place. It will be good for him to have this time with Mary." Nannie spoke in a very direct manner, not leaving room for discussion. "Young Patrick will also accompany you. He has offered to help this evening. He would like to learn about the distillery."

Joseph looked at Grae. "Well, she can do the work." He put his hand on her shoulder, and Grae could smell the whiskey. "I see you made a friend tonight. I wouldn't get too attached to him." Nannie poked Joseph in the arm. "Well, he's a McGavock and she's a…"

"Very interesting young lady sir, I will be honored to learn from you this evening. I know that Arabella is fortunate to be serving someone who is willing for her to learn a skill as well. It will come in handy when her servitude is over."

"Oh, so you know her little secret." Joseph tipped his hat. "We like her." Joseph paused and looked Grae straight in the eye. "She's been good for our family."

Grae felt her eyes well up with tears as she realized that these would probably be his last words to her. She wished that there was some way she could change his fate.

Joseph climbed onto the front of the wagon where Bob was already waiting.

"I shall follow on my horse, Mister Baker. Would you like to ride with me?" Patrick extended his hand to Grae.

She looked at Nannie and then down at her beautiful dress. "Well, I don't want to ruin my dress."

"I assure you that my horse is clean and I believe it would be more comfortable then the back of the wagon."

Grae looked from Nannie to Patrick and then to Joseph. "Go ahead, Belle, ride with Patrick." Nannie said.

Already on the beautiful black horse, Patrick extended his left arm down to Grae. She grabbed hold at the crook of his arm and put her foot into the stirrup. Patrick was so strong that all she had to do was jump up and he pulled her the rest of the way.

The wagon began to move and Grae waved at Nannie. It almost seemed, by the look on her face, that Nannie knew that something was going to happen.

For some reason, the horse wasn't moving. "Are we going to go now or wait until the sun rises?" Patrick might as well learn about her sarcasm too, Grae thought.

"Not until you put your arms around me."

"What?"

"I am not trying to take liberties with you. I just don't want you to fall off. Bob is travelling at a brisk pace, and we will as well if we want to keep up."

Grae slid her arms around Patrick. It was much closer than they had been when they were dancing. She imagined for a moment that this was almost how it would feel to slow dance with Gav at the prom. She hoped she got to do that.

"That's a tight grip you have there. Not that I am complaining. You are not cold, are you?" Since the sun had set, a cool breeze was blowing. She hadn't thought much about it, but she did feel a little chilly. Patrick felt like a muscular electric blanket.

"I'm fine, thank you."

Patrick increased his pace. It seemed as if Bob was getting faster. "Bob is really driving that wagon fast for nighttime."

"I'm sure he knows the way in his sleep. I think he used to work on the Sayers' farm some, a trade with them for some reason."

"That may have been the case, but I doubt he drove a wagon back and forth." Grae leaned around Patrick's shoulder and watched ahead. Without the large moon, it would have been impossible to see the wagon, but the cloud of dust it was leaving made her glad she wasn't in the back of it.

"It would have been a rough ride for me on the back as fast as he is going. Thank you for allowing me to ride with you."

"Oh, Miss Arabella, the pleasure is all mine." Grae felt her face getting warm and was glad that Patrick could not see her blushing. "May I ask you a question?"

"Certainly." Grae was a little afraid as to what this question might be.

"You mentioned earlier that you have two brothers back in England. Will you be going back to care for them when your servitude is over?"

Grae hated that this whole conversation with Patrick was a falsehood, but she didn't see any way around it now. "Well, I haven't really thought that far ahead, but I think that I would rather them come here. America is the land of opportunity. It would be good for them."

"I think that is a wise choice. I believe that my family might be able to help with this. My grandfather's brother is still in England, and he and his son are barristers. We will work to get your brothers reunited with you."

Grae sighed. At that moment, she felt like a fair maiden being rescued by a prince. That feeling didn't last for long as she realized that they were approaching the farm. The barn was lit up with lamps and an old wagon could be seen backed up in front of it. It wasn't hard for Grae to imagine what was happening as they rode closer and saw that the wagon was half full of boxes.

"What are they doing?" Joseph Baker was yelling as he got off the wagon and was almost at the barn before Bob could hardly get the horses stopped.

"I don't understand. Is something wrong?" Patrick had lifted Grae off of his horse and they were standing a dozen feet from the barn's entrance.

To be a relatively small man, Joseph Baker had a very strong voice. It could carry several hundred feet when he was yelling out an order in the fields. When he was angry, his voice could rattle the windows and wake the dead. That was the voice that Grae and Patrick now heard.

Patrick started toward the barn, but Grae grabbed his arm. "Patrick, I think you better go back to the Sayers and get some help."

"No, I will go in there and help Mister Baker. I will protect you."

It took both Grae's hands and all her strength to hold him back. "Patrick, here's what you don't know. Listen to me." Patrick finally stopped and turned toward her. "There are three slaves in there that have been planning to run away. I've heard them talking. This must be the night. I don't know if Bob will stand up to them. He's mighty loyal to Mister Baker, but two of them are his kin. You can't take them all on. We need help. Your horse is fast."

Patrick's face showed the signs of someone wrestling from within. Finally, he looked down at the back of the wagon. He picked up a shotgun that was in the back. He checked to see it was loaded and handed it to Grae. "Do you know how to shoot this?"

"Yes, yes, I do." That was not a lie, although it had been some time. Grandpa Mack had taught both she and Perry how to shoot the previous summer.

"Don't go inside. Shoot this if you have to. Even if you just wound someone, it will slow them down." Patrick stopped in front of Grae and put his hand on her cheek. Ever so lightly, he kissed her. For a moment, she felt dizzy and everything was growing dark. She could have sworn that she was back at the Mansion on that moonlit night and that it was Gav there with her.

The moment was gone. Patrick jumped up on the horse and turned it to the opposite direction.

"I don't feel right about this, but I don't know what else to do. Belle, please be careful. I really want to be able to see you again."

"I will, Patrick, I will. Now, ride fast. Ride like the wind and pray all the way there and back." When she could no longer see him, she turned around and found herself face to face with Sam.

TWENTY ONE

"Massa Baker, you don't understand. We not stealin', we loadin' up this wagon and gettin' it ready for the wagon master. This here barn gettin' too full of whiskey, why someone drop a match and we all go to kingdom come." Aggie spoke in even tones, trying to calm the situation.

"You think I don't know what you are after. You want to run away with that piece of trouble over there. You want to steal from the one who put food in your mouth since you became an orphan. I'm tired of your lies. You are gonna be sold." Joseph took two steps toward Aggie. "You and Sam will be sold and I will see to it that Mister Sayers sells Isaiah. All of you sold in three different directions."

"Now, Massa, you angry and you gots a right to be, but we all calm down and we will finish this work." Bob's steady voice was trembling.

"Don't tell me to calm down. If the overseer was here, I'd have them all taken out back and whipped."

"You not man enough to do it youself." Isaiah uttered his first words. "You got to have the overseer do it." Joseph whirled around at Isaiah.

"Sam not gonna be sold!" Sam's voice thundered over everyone else as he led Grae into the barn, the head of an ax pushing her. "All I wanted was her. I didn't even care whether I was free or not. But you, Aggie, you had to have Isaiah and he wanted to run. So now you got me in all this trouble, stealin' from the Massa, runnin' away, a new life with a bounty on our heads."

Aggie shook her head and kneeled down on the floor as if she was gonna pray.

Sam wasn't finished. "Yes, we be slaves, we born slaves, we die slaves. That's what ole Sal says. But we had it all right. Nobody beat us every day, we have food and a place to sleep. But you had to go and want some no count trouble who all he wanted to do was steal. He didn't want you. He done told the other slaves over there on the Sayers' farm that he was gonna lose you along the way. He got some girl up there in New York waitin' on him. She done had two of his babies."

Aggie rose up and looked in Isaiah's direction. "Tell him he's lyin'. Tell him, Isaiah."

Isaiah came out from a corner. Grae noticed something made of metal in his hand. "You have a better life with me, Aggie. It's a different world up there in the North. We make a good life, all of us together. Don't listen to him. All he sees is that white trash there. Well, you got her, Sam, there she be."

"No, she's not. You all lied to me. Aggie, you said she'd come with us when she figured out that no McGavock gonna want her."

"She will, Sam, her eyes gonna open wide."

Grae could see the anger seething out of Sam. The muscles in his jaw clenched with each word. "How come I just see that young McGavock kissin' her right outside this barn?"

Isaiah started laughing. It was a laugh that started deep inside and grew sinister on its way out. "Well, I guess we gonna have to do this here another way." That piece of steel was now pointed in their direction, it was a gun.

"Old Big Bob, you ain't so tough and you never liked me no way. You got eyes that see the truth, so I be takin' care of that." Quick as a flash, before anyone knew what was happening, Isaiah knocked Bob in the head with the butt of his gun. It didn't take him completely out, but it put the big man down.

Pointing the gun at Joseph Baker, Isaiah started shouting orders. "Sam, you and Aggie tie them two up. Put them on their knees." Sam tied up Joseph first. Isaiah stood behind Joseph with the gun in his back as Aggie began trying to tie Grae. But Grae squirmed and fought. Isaiah aimed the gun for Grae's head.

"I don't want to shoot your pretty head off, but I will." Grae kept squirming, her years of wrestling Perry were finally coming to use. She managed to catch a glimpse of Sam and saw that he now stood behind Isaiah with his ax ready to strike.

Then something unexpected occurred, Joseph Baker began to pray. Speaking out loud with a thunderous voice, the voice he used in the fields, he began to quote Psalm 23. "The Lord is my shepherd; I shall not want. He maketh me to lie down in green pastures; He leadeth me beside the still waters. He restoreth my soul, He leadeth me in the paths of righteousness for his name's sake. Yea, though I walk through the valley of the shadow of death, I will fear no evil; for thou art with me; thy rod and thy staff they comfort me."

It was as if everyone was spellbound for a moment, thinking about those words. All, but one person, the reality of the situation returned as Isaiah released the safety on the gun. The anger was raging out of Sam like the sweat on his forehead. He heard a gunshot and his ax went down. Isaiah fell to the ground, hit by a bullet, and the head of the ax went straight through Joseph Baker's skull.

Grae screamed. Sam let go of the ax and looked behind him. The gunshot had come from the gun Grae had dropped when Sam brought her inside. The gun that Patrick gave her was now in his own hands.

From then on everything was in slow motion to Grae. Bob crawled over to Joseph Baker and turned him over. It was a horrible sight.

"Lawd, what you done, boy? Lawd, what you done?"

Joseph's face was hardly recognizable. His white Sunday shirt was covered in his own red blood.

Aggie just sat in a corner and rocked back and forth as she stared at Isaiah lying on the ground. The dirt was turning red all around him. His blood, the blood of Joseph Baker, all mixed together in death.

As Grae tried to focus on Patrick standing there with the gun in his hand, she saw Nannie come out from the shadows behind him. She raised her hands up to the sky and shouted. "Why? Why, God, why?"

Kneeling next to him, she pulled her husband's lifeless body into her lap as Bob kept saying over and over again. "It's my fault. I shoulda stopped it. It's my fault."

The men of the community were soon there. Not knowing what happened they loaded up Bob, Sam, Aggie, and Grae and took them all off to be shackled in the basement of the Baker's cabin. They were all slaves, servants, owned. They were all guilty.

Patrick stood in shock as Grae was taken with the rest of them. "I'll see you again," Grae said to Patrick as she was led away. "We will be together again someday."

TWENTY TWO

After the first night when they were all held in the basement, she and Aggie were moved away from Sam and Bob. She didn't know where Aggie was taken, but Grae was put in a very small stone room that was part of the basement, but had a small window. Grae's shackles were attached on her right foot, so all she could do was sit and stare out of the tiny window. Its view was obstructed further by three metal bars, but at least there was light and air in the dank, dark space.

On the morning of her third day in confinement, the heavy wooden door opened. Grae burst into tears as she saw Sal maneuver her large self into the tiny space. She sat down as the door was closed and the sound of the lock made her jump. Sal looked as if there was no more crying in her. She was a shell of her former self. Her big eyes had a blankness to them that could only be understood as grief.

"Belle girl, it pains me to sees you in this awful place in chains. Bob has told and told them that you didn't have no such thing to do with it. Mister Patrick done told the same thing, buts they thinks he be sweet on you and would tell a story."

Grae looked down at Sal's hands and her fingers were bleeding from the nervous winding of a handkerchief around her fingers over and over again. White cloth, red blood, would she ever get that image out of her head.

"I comes to see my Bob and Aggie and I comes to see you." Sal paused and looked down at her hands. "I hopes that you might write a letter for me. I send to my sista, she owned by a man who be a lawyer. Maybe she talk to him about comin' and helpin' us."

"I will write the letter." It seemed to Grae that those five words took a whole lot of strength to get out. "You brought paper?"

"I did. I broughts that tablet and pencil that Massa Baker," Sal started crying, "that he, God rest his soul, gives for you to teach me on."

"What about Sam? What's happened to him?"

"Oh, he be in a bad state. He not said one word since it happened. He just stare. I went in to see him and he not even nod his head at me. He just look at his hands like they don't belong to him. I guess he wish they didn't. They killin' hands now. That boy done dead already. I just hopes my Bob don't have to go with him."

Grae began writing the basics of the story and also a few other things that Sal wanted to tell her sister. After she finished and Sal had signed her name, Grae had an idea. "How's Missus Baker doing?"

"Oh Lawd, she just sits in her rocking chair and goes back and forth. She not hardly said two words. All her chil'en are huddled around her and doing the business of the house. She just sits there. They buried Massa Baker yesterday. She told Massa Charlie to comes and gets me. I stood right behind her as they puts him in the ground. All the white folks just glared at me, but I stand tall behind her. We be together for a lifetime." Sal stopped and let out a big sigh. "She turned to me after it over and says she know it weren't Bob, but he was there and he probably gonna have to pay."

"What does Bob say?"

"My Bob he filled with guilt. He says it don't matter what happens to him, living or dead, he gonna walk the land of that farm forever. He says his soul be cursed." Sal shook her head. "Massa Baker, he owned us, Belle, ain't no denyin' that. It be the way of the world. Somebody be owner, somebody be slave. But we all be like family. Somebody might as well have kilt my Bob, he already be dead. No denyin' that Sam he used that ax. Lawd, I wish it hit the one that it was meant for. Then only one man be dead, the one that should be. Now two be dead and two more will be soon." Sal looked up at Grae. "And I don't know what gonna happen to you and to Aggie. I just don't know."

"Sal, you sit there a minute and pull yourself together. I'm going to write another letter, and I want you to give it to Missus Baker."

Sal left a little while later and the rest of the day drug on. In the early evening, Grae heard some commotion. It sounded like the others were being moved, but it was very loud. Grae also heard a cat meowing and started to think she was losing her mind until she saw a paw coming through the bars on the window, followed by the rest of the body and a tail. It was The General.

"What are you doing here?" Grae tried to jump up and remember that movement was hindered.

"You've got to get out of here. They are moving the rest of them to another location."

"I know I need to get out of here, but I don't see how that can happen with me shackled to the floor and in a stone cell."

"No, Grae, you don't understand. You are still on the Mansion's acreage, the land of your time. They are going to move you off that land. If you are off the land, you will not be able to travel back. If you are locked in some prison cell miles from here, you will be stuck in this time. You've got to get out of 1786."

"How in the world do I do that?"

The General flipped his tail up in the air. "You unlock yourself from the time the way you would unlock yourself anywhere. You use a key."

Grae reached for her neck and found the leather cord that held her key. She had almost forgotten it was still with her. The General had told her that the reason it travelled with her was because it was from this time. Could it really be so simple that this key fit the lock on her shackles?

"Before you do that, I must say goodbye."

"But you are coming with me, I know you live on the Mansion property."

"That I do, but in your time we cannot communicate. You will see me, but we shall not talk. It is against the rules."

"So, I'll never get to talk to you again? I'll miss you. You have been my best friend."

"Well, Grae, the thing about time travel is," The General laughed, "it's like potato chips, once you start eating, you can't stop. I imagine that you will travel again, and if you do, I will go with you."

"How will I know when it's time?"

"You are a seeker of truth. That is your purpose. You will find mysteries that must be solved, questions that demand answers, just as you have found on this journey. You will know when and, now, you also know how to get here. You know where your portal is that will lead you to the chosen point in time. But, it will not always be that simple. Just like that key fits this lock, each time you travel there will be an object that you must carry with you to help you return. Be careful to bring the right one. Goodbye, Grae." The General climbed back out through the window then turned and stuck his head back through the bars. "And don't be so hard on Perry. It's not easy being the little brother."

The noise outside her door grew louder, Grae knew she didn't have much time. She took the key from around her neck. As she reached for the lock, she looked around that tiny room, her cell. She needed to remember this experience; she needed to soak it up for the future. As the lock on the wooden door began to click, she slid her key into the lock on her shackles and turned it.

Everything began to spin. A shrill sound filled her ears. Everything began tilting and Grae felt herself falling. Two hundred years was pulling at her, from the outside, from the inside, like an unseen force tearing her apart. She reached for something to hold onto, even knowing that nothing was there. She saw swirls of green and purple mist all around her and Patrick's face smiling in the fog, or was it Gav? The air smelled different this time, like the sterile cold oxygen from a hospital mask. She tried to say something, but all she could hear was the shrieking and all she could feel was the speed of time. Just when she thought it would never end, everything went black.

PRESENT DAY

TWENTY THREE

With a thump, Grae landed on the floor of the closet in the Mansion. When everything stopped spinning, she realized she was still wearing the beautiful dress that Nannie and Mary had made her. She kept looking at it in amazement. Why had this dress travelled with her?

Slowly, she rose and walked into the hallway. Turning back, she looked at the simple old closet and thought about its power. She wondered what had happened within the walls to transform the forgotten space into a time travel portal. As she caught her reflection in the foyer mirror, reality hit her hard. Somehow she was going to have to explain not only her change in appearance, but also her change in demeanor. Seeing two people die inches away had changed her. Living the life of a servant in a forgotten century had given her a perspective that her fellow teens would never understand. The days of imprisonment had carved a niche into her soul that made her personal desire for teenage freedom seem irrelevant, but gave the plight of her father a whole new meaning.

Grae looked at the clock and tried to make sense of what day it was. If time had not passed in the present, as The General said, then it was still Sunday and her mother's list of cleaning tasks weren't finished. Grandpa Mack and Perry could be home at any moment. Her mother would return from Charlotte in the early evening. She must get out of the dress and hide it somewhere, cleanup, and do something about her hair.

The shower was like a thousand heavens. She vowed to research the inventor of the whole concept and sing the praises of this creative genius. As she let the hot steaming water relax her tired body, she couldn't help but conjure images of the month she had spent in another time. It was a dull distant feeling that was sharp around the edges. This feeling might be kindred to having lost a very close loved one. She felt now like her mother had looked when Grae's grandmother had passed. The feeling reminded her of a balloon which had lost all its air and was left flailing in its last bit of strength.

She thought of Joseph Baker, who had died two hundred years before, but only a few days ago in her mind. Had she really touched the lives of these people? Maybe it was all just a very bad dream; maybe something had happened to her sanity. As her washcloth passed over the infinity symbol on the underside of her right hand, she realized that her sanity was indeed intact. She had experienced another time, another world. She had been given a rare opportunity to find truth in tragedy.

Her mind wandered to a happier memory, a gentle one. She smiled thinking about Patrick. He was like all she knew of Gav, and all she had yet to discover. His gentle kiss warmed her soul. She knew at that moment that Gav was not going to be a normal teenage boyfriend. He was going to be her soul mate. She would tuck that information safe inside her heart and enjoy their young time together.

After dressing in shorts and a t-shirt, Grae put the key, now back on its gold chain, around her neck. She didn't know if it would take her anywhere else, but liked the security of knowing it was with her.

She hung the dress on a hanger. Being as long as it was, she had gotten used to it being a little heavy, but as she was adjusting it, she noticed that it was pulling down on one side. Looking under the bottom of the dress, she saw that there was a small pocket sewed into a spot right above the hem. She wondered why she hadn't noticed it before and then realized that whatever was in the pocket was close to the same weight as the heavy bows that had been placed every eight to ten inches apart near the bottom of the dress. The pretty decoration had hidden a secret.

Opening the pocket, she saw that the object inside appeared to be wrapped in paper. As she unwrapped it, she noticed it had the appearance of age that would have passed during the journey. It was another strange memento from travelling through time. The hidden object was a very small pocket knife; its handle had a green jade tint to it and the initials J.J.B. were engraved on it. Examining the piece of paper, she realized that there were words on it. The aged handwriting was hard to make out, but Grae thought it read, "Thought you might need this for your next visit. Joseph will not need it now. Hope to see you another time. Mary."

Grae read the words over and over. Mary must have sewn it into her dress days before her father-in-law died, but how did she know? Grae wondered if that reference to 'another time' meant in another time. Could Mary be a time traveler herself?

Grae examined the knife more closely. It appeared to be well crafted and expensive. Perhaps it had been a gift from someone close to Joseph Baker. Grae wondered how Mary had gotten possession of it. She would need to keep it in a very safe place. Looking closer, she realized that there was a small ring on the end. She could probably attach a string or fine chain to it and keep it with the key. Grae laughed; if she went on many more adventures she would have an anchor around her neck. It felt good to laugh, to let her emotions be slightly light-hearted for a few moments. It was going to be hard to hide what she had experienced, almost as hard as hiding her hair.

She wasn't sure what had happened to the bow that she had worn the night of the murder. It probably had been knocked off during her scuffle with Aggie and Isaiah. All the pins that had hidden her hair's shortness had disappeared as well. Grae shook her wet head like a dog and looked in the mirror. Viewing from several angles, she realized that she actually didn't look half bad in a short cut, but how would she explain getting a haircut on a Sunday afternoon?

Grae decided that some fresh 21st century air would help her clear her head. She walked outside and took in the mountain landscape. It was amazing how different it appeared now. She didn't just see its scenic beauty, now she saw its years of history, happiness, and heartache. It was as if the land could speak to her now, and she knew it had more stories to tell.

As she soaked up everything around her in a moment of quiet, the loud voice of an idea came to her from behind the Mansion. "Shakespeare! Where are you? Mama's got your din din."

"Oh, yes, that will work!" Grae ran around the side of the Mansion toward the white house that sat beside it, up on the hill. It had been the caretaker's house a decade or two previously, but he died before Grandpa retired. Now it was the home of the owner's "crazy cousin" as he affectionately described her. She was actually the daughter of his favorite cousin and she just happened to also cut hair.

"Hey, Lucy, whatcha' doing?"

"Hey, Grae, have you seen Shakespeare?" Lucy's dog was a cross between a Schnauzer and a Poodle. Grae called him a "Schnoodle."

"No, Lucy, I haven't, but I've been gone for a while." Grae walked up onto the porch. The white paint on the steps was peeling and revealed that it had once been a weird shade of yellow. "I was wondering if you could cut my hair."

Lucy walked around and looked at Grae's hair. "Good grief, girl, it looks like somebody already did."

"Well, it was an attempt, but as you can see, it wasn't a good one. I really need a professional to fix it."

"Well, I don't know about the professional part," Lucy ran her hands through her own hair; this week it was red, "but I have cut on a few heads in my day."

Lucy's choice of words always amazed Grae, but considering the circumstances, they were unusually accurate. "Do you think you can fix it? Mom will be home soon and I don't think she will be happy. I have prom next week."

"Well, in that case, we have just got to take this disaster and make it into a movie." Grae wasn't exactly sure what Lucy meant, but the forty-something crazy lady seemed to be serious. At this point, Grae didn't think she had much to lose.

Lucy was chatty for the first half hour that Grae was in her chair, but then as she began mixing a hair rinse potion, as she called it, she seemed to be in deep concentration. She wouldn't let Grae watch as she did her work, so Grae was forced to look at the walls of the room that Lucy used as her hair studio. On one wall were the standard posters that could be seen in lots of beauty salons; beautiful models with perfect hair touting all the latest products and looking as if they had never experienced a bad hair day. That wall made Grae sick, so she moved on to another wall. This one was dedicated to Elvis from Tupelo to the Great Beyond. Grae didn't know a lot about the King of Rock & Roll, but she could certainly tell that Lucy held him in great esteem. So it surprised her that throughout the whole hour that she had already been in Lucy's chair, she had only heard songs from the 80s, like Prince and Madonna.

"So, Lucy, why is Elvis on the wall, but not on your iPod?" Grae noticed a pretty purple iPod docked in the corner.

"That's a very observant question, Grae." Lucy went back to working on Grae's hair.

A few more minutes passed without an answer, Grae didn't want to make anyone this close to her with hair dye angry, but she really wanted to know why. "No Elvis downloads on your playlist?"

"Well, Grae, it's just too painful to listen." Lucy put her hand to her heart and sniffed back a tear. Grae decided that perhaps it was best to leave that subject alone. The lapse of silence ended as Lucy twirled the chair around, and Grae could see herself in the mirror.

Grae gasped. Lucy had turned the choppy cut into all sorts of layers and wisps. "How did you get the color to do that?" Grae's dark hair normally had an almost blue hue to it, but now the tips had a silver sheen, like they were dipped in glitter.

"Well, I really don't know. Your hair looked like it had been in a fight, so I thought it might be good to give it a little color rinse that matched your natural shade. It seemed fine until I began evening up that crazy cutting job you had. Each place that I cut, the tip turned silver." Lucy walked around and faced Grae. "Now, honey, you can tell me, have you been taking any drugs?"

Grae laughed out loud and shook her head. "Oh, it must be those time-released vitamins I've been taking."

Lucy shrugged. "Well, that doesn't sound right, but you never know these days. I really think that all these preservatives in foods are mind-controlling substances. You don't seem like the druggie type. Your skin's too clear."

Another statement from Lucy that didn't quite make sense, but at least she wasn't asking lots of probing questions. Grae continued to stare at her hair in the mirror. It really was a neat look. It would turn some heads at the Prom. She couldn't help but wonder what had happened to her hair to make it do this. She wondered what else she would find out about herself as the next few days and weeks passed.

"I appreciate your help, Lucy. You really saved me today. How much do I owe you?" Grae stood up and Shakespeare jumped into the seat. "Guess you found Shakespeare."

"Oh, you don't owe me a thing Grae, glad to help. We all need to help each other hide things from time to time, especially when the truth is nothing but scary." Once again Lucy's words were hauntingly accurate. Perhaps Lucy wasn't crazy; she just saw things that others didn't take the time to realize.

TWENTY FOUR

For the next couple of hours, Grae hurriedly worked on the remaining cleaning assignments that her mother had left. While it wasn't as thorough as Kat probably wanted, each of the areas did look shiny. The work seemed very easy to Grae now. Having all of the modern day tools and products made a world of difference. Her attitude toward cleaning would forever be nicer. It was easy to clean in this century.

"Hey, Grae, where are you?" Perry shouted from the back of the house.

"In the front room, on the right!" Grae shouted back. She took a deep breath and prepared herself for this encounter. She had really missed her family and, at some points, wondered if she would ever see them again. She had to try not to let these emotions show. She was working on cleaning the windows, so at least she could keep focused on that and not look at Perry for too long.

"You should see the huge bass that Grandpa caught," Perry said as he barreled into the room. He stopped short as he saw Grae. "Oh, my gosh, what have you done to your hair? Mom is going to kill you."

Perry seemed a little taller somehow. Grae remembered The General's words as a sarcastic comment waited in her mouth. She touched the back of her head. "I just wanted a change. What do you think?"

A look passed through Perry's eyes. "Well, Sis, you said you wanted something different for the prom. That's different." Perry walked closer and looked at her from different angles. "As much as I hate to admit it, it really looks good on you. Gav will think it's hot."

Perry's compliment touched her heart and she enveloped him into a huge hug. He seemed to feel awkward at first, but then hugged back.

"Grae! We got anything to eat around here? The hungry fishermen are home." Grandpa Mack came walking through the hallway. As Grae and Perry walked into the hallway to meet him, Grae saw that he had stopped in front of the closet.

"What have you been doing in there?" The look on Grandpa Mack's face was unusual. It almost looked like a mixture of anger and fear.

"Well, I was just cleaning it out. That was on Mom's list of things for me to do."

"Well, I guess that's okay. There's just a lot of old stuff in there. You don't need to be staying in there too long, it's dangerous."

"Dangerous, Grandpa?" Perry asked. "It's just an old closet."

"Well, son, that's what it may look like, but that's not what it has always been." Grandpa turned and walked back toward the kitchen. "I'm hungry."

Grae could tell by his tone that this conversation was over, but she wondered if he had just given her a big clue as to why that closet could transcend time.

It was almost dark by the time Kat returned. To Grae, this had been the longest day of her life. She knew she needed to keep this journey a secret from her mother; but she really wondered if that would be possible.

Grandpa Mack and Perry had already gone to bed. Their energy drained from a long day in the hot sun. After Grae fixed hamburgers, the two of them snored in the chairs in the living room until they finally surrendered. Grae sat on the porch and watched the sun set. It was a deep orange red, but Grae was afraid that the color would forever hold a different meaning for her. Red now symbolized something somber to Grae. Somehow she would need to find a way to give the color a positive meaning again.

With a queasy feeling in her stomach, she watched as her mother pulled into the driveway in the old black Jeep. As she walked toward the vehicle, her mother got out. Silhouetted in the setting sun, her mother looked younger somehow, or maybe it was Grae that now saw her with different eyes. She realized that those feelings of mother-daughter animosity were not present in her heart now. Grae saw her mother as a kindred spirit, and she wished that she could know of her experiences. She wasn't sure that her mother would share those with her. She realized they would be hard to verbalize and might even recount memories Kat would just as soon not recall.

As Grae came into her view, Kat's eyes grew large. "Oh my, you've had an interesting day."

Grae laughed softly at her mother's statement. It seemed as if everyone now had an undertone of irony. Grae wondered if this would be her new normal.

"Yes, I have." Grae paused and took a package out of her mother's arms. "It was eventful, but I completed my tasks." Another statement with double meanings and this time it came out of Grae's mouth.

"I don't remember writing the words 'drastic hairstyle change' on my list this morning."

"Oh, I ended up deviating from your list for a while. Change seemed appropriate." She followed her mother into the Mansion and placed the packages in the foyer. Grae had carefully returned items to the closet and closed the door, but it still gave her a strange feeling to look toward it.

"Oh my, this is a big change." Grae turned to find her mother examining her hair. "How did you get this done on a Sunday afternoon? What's that color on the ends? Did you have it tipped?"

"Lucy helped me."

"Well, that explains a lot. Really, Grae, you could have waited, I would have taken you to a real salon."

Grae paused and thought about what her mother just said. Deciding not to reply, she turned and went back to the Jeep for another load. Her mother followed.

"It's really kind of a drastic thing to do the week before the Prom. I wished you would have waited and discussed it with me."

Grae quickly turned, facing her mother. "There are a lot of things I wished you had discussed with me." Arms loaded, Grae briskly walked with another load. Her mother followed, empty-handed.

"Now, Grae, if this is about your father, you know that there was nothing I could do to prevent what happened."

"No," Grae said, still walking, "but you could have given us a little more warning about this move and where we were going."

Grae wasn't sure why she was bringing up the move, but at least it got them off the real topic for a few moments. The last load was now in her arms. Kat slammed the back door of the Jeep shut.

"Grae, we had no choice, this was the only place we had to go."

"I'm not talking about choices; I know the situation Dad left us in. I said warning. Perry and I had no idea how fast everything was moving. It seemed like the trial went on forever. Then all of a sudden, we are packing a U-Haul and moving here."

Kat let out a big sigh. "Well, there was a lot going on. I guess I just tried to handle things and keep you and your brother from having to be in all of it."

"But that's the point, Mom, we were in it anyway. It would have been nice to know what was coming." Grae realized that she was not just talking about the move, but she wasn't sure that her mother could handle the rest of the story right now. "Grandpa Mack and Perry went to bed a while ago. They had a successful day of fishing. I'm tired too, I'm going to bed." Grae began walking up the staircase.

"Grae, honey, I think you hair looks cute. I'm sorry I snapped at you. You are old enough to make these decisions without me. It will look great with your dress."

"Oh, I've changed my mind about the dress I'm wearing." Grae was still climbing the stairs.

"Grae, we can't afford to buy another dress. What's wrong with the one we bought?"

"I found one I like better and it didn't cost any money." Once she was at her doorway, she whispered to herself. "Just a piece of my soul."

TWENTY FIVE

Grae and Perry left for school the following morning without much discussion about the previous day. As she walked down the hallways, Grae was met with some double takes and stares, but they were teenagers, they all did weird things. She found Carrie standing at her locker.

"Wow! That's like a major dramatic change there. Your mom didn't say anything about you getting your hair cut."

"It happened while you all were gone to Charlotte." Even though time had stood still while she was in 1786, Grae found it hard to use the word yesterday.

"That certainly made your Sunday afternoon different." Carrie watched as Perry walked past. "Hey, this is kind of last minute and maybe a crazy idea…." Somehow Grae imagined that nothing Carrie could say would surprise her after the journey. Carrie moved closer to Grae and began to whisper. "I was wondering if you could get Perry to be my date to the prom." Except maybe what she just said.

"What? Perry? The prom?" Grae was having trouble imagining Perry in a tux, or a tie, or shoes that didn't have white laces.

"Yeah, um, well, I kind of have been thinking about it for a while, but I didn't know how to approach him."

"Good grief, just ask him." Grae heard the tone of her voice. She was really going to have to lighten up and shake this two hundred year-old dust from her attitude. "I'm sorry; you want me to talk to him, don't you?" Carrie looked up shyly and shook her head. "Okay, I guess we better do that quickly. Getting him a tuxedo might be hard at this late hour." Grae looked around. "Go away."

"I didn't mean to make you mad, Grae. Just forget it. I can go alone."

"No, I mean go away so I can ask Perry. You don't want to be standing here when I do it, do you?"

"Oh, gosh, no, absolutely not." Carrie gave Grae a big smile. "You're the best!"

"Yeah, well, let's see what he says first. Hey, Perry, come here." Carrie quickly scampered in the opposite direction from where Perry was coming. She looked back once and began walking even faster.

"What's up, Crew Cut?" Perry gave Grae a huge toothy grin.

"Ah, for that, you are going to have to say yes to what I am about to ask you or face the consequences." Grae returned the grin.

"I will not do your home chores so that you can get other crazy things done to your body this week." Perry leaned on the locker next to Grae, almost stepping on a girl sitting nearby.

"That's not what I was going to ask. How would you like to go to the prom?"

"What? Did Gav take one look at the new hairdo and ditch you? I don't know whether to laugh or go beat him up." Grae laughed, Perry was many things, but always her brother.

"No, I haven't even seen Gav today."

"Oh, but he's seen you." Gav came up behind them. "And he's heard about the girl with the really short hair." Gav said.

Grae slowly turned around and gazed up at him. It seemed as if it had been months since she had seen him and yesterday at the same time. Without thinking, she jumped up and hugged him.

"Hey, man, what's up?" Perry tried to be cool around Gav. "Grae went all scissor crazy on us yesterday while me and Gramps were fishing. We caught some major…"

"I think the cut is almost as cute as Grae." Grae saw Patrick for an instant as Gav lowered her to the floor from the hug. She tried to divert attention from herself by continuing her conversation with her brother.

"Perry, what I was trying to ask you was if you would like to be Carrie's date to the prom?" Grae knew that it probably wasn't the best idea to be asking Perry in front of Gav for Carrie's sake. He might decide to torture her with it later, but she also knew that Perry wouldn't turn the idea down in front of Gav either.

"Ah, well," Perry was stalling and that gave Gav time to get into the conversation.

"Carrothead? What are you asking him that for?" Gav seemed a little put off by the question.

"Carrie doesn't have a date to the prom."

"Well, she should have come to me. I could get one of my guys to be her date. Any one of the junior class who wants to play sports next year would not turn me down. You don't have to ask your brother."

Grae put her hand on Gav's arm. In a split second, she saw Patrick again and his vest of buttons in front of her. Letting go, the image disappeared. Grae shook her head, blinking her eyes several times.

"She wants Perry to be her date."

"She does?" Perry and Gav said simultaneously.

"Yes, she does."

"Well, I think I can do that," Perry said smiling. "Oh, but how am I going to get a tux?"

"We will have to go right after school and see if we can place a last minute order." Grae took her first period books out of her locker. "Okay, that's it. You are excused." Perry turned and started to walk away. "Oh, wait a minute, Perry, if you see Carrie today, be nice and speak to her. It will be good practice for Saturday night." Perry rolled his eyes and walked off.

"I don't believe what I just heard. My sister is going to the prom with your brother." Gav was standing in the middle of the hallway shaking his head. "I just never imagined that my sister would ever actually like a guy. I mean, well, she's my little sister."

"Oh, Gav, get your head out of the sand. Your sister is 16. She is going to like some guys. I've got to admit, it does surprise me that it is Perry that she has chosen, but hey, it will be really interesting for us to watch." They were now in front of their first period class. "I don't think I know what color her dress is. I'll need to know that to do Perry's tux order."

"Speaking of dress colors, I know your secret. I heard Mom talking to someone on the phone about your purple dress." Gav seemed pleased with himself.

"Oh yeah, I guess I better order something for you too. I'm not wearing that dress. I've got another one."

"What? I thought once you girls found the perfect dress there was no turning back."

Grae thought for a moment before she answered. "Let's just say that my style has changed a little."

"I'll say!" Gav looked at her hair. "I'm a little afraid to think about what might happen between now and Saturday."

"You're not the only one."

TWENTY SIX

The next few days were a flurry of activity. Kat was spending most of her time getting the downstairs of the Mansion ready for the After Prom and preparing all of the food that could be made in advance. She noticed that Grae was a little distant, but imagined that it was all the excitement of the week ahead. All of Kat's careful planning did make her Wednesday plans possible, a quiet surprise for Grae.

Grae wasn't too surprised to see Gav and Carrie at the Mansion when she came home Wednesday evening. It was just a couple of nights before the prom, and Grae imagined that her mother was calling in a lot of helpers for last minute decorating. But the way that they were sitting on the porch with Perry and Grandpa Mack was a little weird, like they were waiting for her.

"Hey, did Mom let you all have a break from decorating?" They all exchanged glances.

"Yes, that's right." Perry said. "She gave us a few minutes to de-Zombie ourselves. Can I help you with that?" Grae was carrying a long hanging bag. "Is that my tux?"

"No, it isn't your tux, it's my dress. I just picked it up from the cleaners." Everyone, but Grandpa, stood up as if they were going to open the bag.

"Oooh, let's see it!" Carrie said.

"No, not until Saturday night." Grae had especially requested that the dress be placed in a protective bag that could not be seen through. She was glad that she did. She hardly expected an audience when she came home.

Grae walked through the doorway as her mother was heading to the door. "Hello dear, so glad you are home." Kat looked at the bag Grae was carrying. "What is that?"

"The dress I am wearing to the prom. I had it dry-cleaned."

"Oh, wonderful, let's look at it."

"No, not now."

"Very well, you go and put it in your room, and then come back downstairs. I need you to help me in the dining room."

As Grae hung the dress in her closet, she noticed that there was a note attached to the outside of the bag. "We found something in the dress, but we returned it to the pocket after cleaning." Grae started to take the dress out of the bag and see what was there.

"GRAE!" Her mother yelled from downstairs. "Hurry up."

"Okay!" Grae let go of the dress and closed the door. "I'll look for it later," she said to herself.

When Grae returned to the dining room, everyone yelled, "Surprise!" With everything that had recently transpired, Grae honestly had forgotten what day it was, that it was actually May 10, her 18th birthday. Everyone sat around the table as her mother served her favorite meal, one of her mother's specialties, Pad Thai.

"I knew it had been a while since you had your favorite. So while we were in Charlotte, I got all the ingredients. I thought we would have a nice quiet dinner with family and friends."

Grae smiled. This was how every one of she and Perry's birthdays had been. There might be a party with other children before or after the actual day, but their birthdays were always for family. It was good that some things had not changed.

As Kat was getting ready to serve dessert, the phone rang. Grandpa Mack answered it and called for Grae. He was holding his hand over the mouthpiece when Grae came to answer.

"It's a collect call from your father. Do you want me to accept it?"

First, she hadn't remembered it was her birthday. Then she hadn't even considered hearing from her father. Perhaps her mind was too overloaded from all she had experienced in 1786, or maybe she had aged on the journey. Grae shook her head yes, and Grandpa Mack accepted the call. Taking a deep breath, she answered.

"Hello."

"Hey, there, Sunshine, happy birthday! Gosh, I wish I could be there to give you a big hug." In the background, Grae could hear the sound of people shouting.

"Thanks, Dad, I appreciate you calling me."

"Well, I couldn't miss my girl's big birthday. Are you doing anything special?"

"Mom fixed my favorite dinner."

"Pad Thai."

"Yes, that's right. It was delicious."

"It always was."

"And a couple of my school friends are here."

"Are any of them boys?"

"Well, yes, I have a boyfriend, sort of. We are going to the prom on Saturday night."

"Now I hope you aren't running around with some redneck hillbilly. You can do better than that, Grae." Grae held the phone away from her and shook her head.

"Always have an opinion, don't you, Dad?"

"Well, I don't want my little girl getting mixed up with any troublemakers."

"I'll try not to take after my mother."

"Graham Belle, that is no way to talk to me. I'm innocent, you know that."

"My boyfriend has never been in jail, if that is what you are worried about. He has all his teeth and has been offered several athletic scholarships to some great universities. I don't think he will be joining you in your present location."

"Grae, I didn't mean anything by that. I just wanted to…"

"Control my life like you always tried to control Mom's. Thanks for calling, Dad."

"Let me talk to your mother. I want her to bring you and Perry to see me soon."

"That's okay, Dad, it won't be necessary. We are doing just fine."

"Grae, you don't understand what it is like to be imprisoned. They even make us do manual labor without pay."

"Actually, Dad, I do understand. There are a lot of things you are just going to miss. But you made your choice, now you will have to pay the consequences. Bye, Dad."

Grae hung up the phone before anything else could be said. She turned and saw Perry standing behind her. "I'm sorry, Perry; I should have let you talk to him. He just made me so mad." Perry put his arm around Grae.

"It's okay. I think I understand now. Grandpa showed me all the newspaper articles and told me lots of things that I guess I just refused to see and understand. He cheated a lot of people, including us. We will all be fine."

Grae buried her head in her brother's chest and gave him a big hug. He was towering over her now.

"Now, let's eat cake."

The rest of the evening was very enjoyable for Grae. Eating cake, laughing with her friends, and Grandpa Mack telling stories about when she was little. It was all great fun. After Carrie and Gav left, Grandpa Mack told Perry to help his mother clean things up, and he took Grae into the living room. Next to his chair was a long box, wrapped in white paper and a big red bow. At first the sight startled her, but when she heard where it came from, the color slipped away.

"Grandpa, you already gave me a present. I love the card and the money."

"Darling, this is not from me. Sit down on the couch, and I will tell you a story." Grae sat down on the long couch and her grandfather sat beside her as he placed the box on her lap. "That summer that you spent with us before your grandmother got sick is one of my favorite memories. But for your grandmother, it was her last wonderful experience. After that, she got her diagnosis, and she knew that she would probably not be around for today. In your grandmother's time, turning 18 was a big deal. Many girls got married at 18 and began starting families. It was really when they crossed into adulthood. That may be different now, but she wanted you to have something that would signify your ability to start a new chapter in your life." Grandpa wiped his eyes and kissed Grae on the forehead. "What's in that box was made with her own two hands, and she made me promise that I would wait and give it to you today. I never even told your mother about it until yesterday. I'm gonna leave you alone now, because this is your time with her. Goodnight, Grae Belle, happy birthday."

Tears were streaming down her face as Grae watched her grandfather hobble out of the room. Somehow, this man she always knew as a mighty ox now didn't look so strong. Grief has a way of taking the life out of a person.

She patted the box and played with the bow as she took a deep breath. She carefully opened the package, wanting to savor every moment of this time with her beloved grandmother. She knew that there would be very few moments in life like this; the chance to connect with someone long since gone away.

She pulled off the top of the box and saw that there was an envelope on top of the tissue paper. It had been carefully attached with tiny straight pins to the paper. It was obvious that her grandmother wanted her to read this before she dug into the gift. A sob caught in Grae's throat as she opened it and saw her grandmother's beautiful handwriting. Only days before, she had seen it on countless documents in her research, but after her journey, this personal touch had new meaning.

"My Dear Grae Belle,

If you are reading this letter, then I suppose I have passed on, as I would have said these things to you in person if I was there for your special day. I wanted to make sure that if I could not physically be with you on your 18th birthday, I still could be a part of it somehow.

I realized during that special summer, that you and I are more alike than I imagined. You have that spunky spirit that makes you want to know the 'whys' of life. I was that way myself for more years than I thought possible. I probably would have stayed that way my entire lifetime, if I had not had to face such great sadness during the middle time of my life.

As the years pass, you will learn many things about your family and yourself. Every family has its secrets, and we are no exception. Many of ours have been hidden for too long. You need to be a seeker of truth and dig deep into our mysteries. You will have a taste for adventure. You will want to learn the truth behind a mystery. Maybe you can help someone along the way. Remember, Grae, helping someone can take many forms and is not stifled by the hands of time. It's never too late to right a wrong, even if everyone involved is long since departed. Perhaps as you make this journey, you will learn some things about yourself along the way.

Now, I will tell you a special story to help explain your gift. Many years ago, when your grandfather and I were a young couple, we helped the owners of the Mansion do a massive cleanup and remodel of sorts. It was a huge project, and it took many months and lots of money. There were so many upgrades that needed to be made; it took dozens of men to do all the work. I didn't want to be too far from your grandfather, so I went to the Mansion every day and helped in any way I could. It was during that time that your mother started growing inside me. It was a very special time.

One of the most interesting things about the Mansion is that it is a house within a house, a story within a story. There were additions added through the years, and several distinct family groups who lived there. If you remember from the research we worked on together, the first family was the Bakers. They lived in a log cabin that was always believed to have been built on the same plot of ground on which the Mansion now stands. A lot of people have doubted that a portion of the present Mansion was constructed around the Baker cabin, but during that remodel I learned the truth.

As they were working on some of the electricity for the house, one of the workmen found a wall within a wall. The hidden wall was log and appeared to date back to the mid-1700s. Lodged between two of the logs was a heavy burlap bag. Inside the bag was cotton cloth. There were several different colors and patterns rolled within each other. Amazingly the fabric was in pretty good shape. The men gave me the fabric. I put it away in an old trunk and forgot about it for many years. But after our time together, I remembered it and thought it was time to put it to use. As I unrolled all the many pieces, I found a letter within it. It is in the bottom of this box. Perhaps it will give you some insight into a mystery that has long since been forgotten. Perhaps it will be the key for a seeker of truth to bring closure for some lost souls.

I love you very much, my dear, and I will always be with you. Be true to yourself and listen to your heart. Most of all, embrace adventure, it can take you beyond your imagination."

Grae smiled behind her tears. It was amazing how her grandmother knew exactly what to tell her, long before she needed to know it. She pulled the tissue back and took out a large quilt. The underside was visible and on the white cloth, she saw the intricate stitching of her grandmother's hand. As she opened it, she saw that it was a beautiful flower garden design with prints and solids in a variety of colors. Looking closely, she gasped as she realized that the same fabric of her 1786 dress made by Nannie and Mary was also in the material of this exquisite quilt. As she continued to study it, she realized that she recognized other pieces of fabric as being from dresses Nannie, Mary, and even Sal had worn. She pulled the quilt toward her and cried into it. Tears of sadness, of joy, of loss; all the emotions that had developed from the love she felt for her friends from another time.

With the quilt over her lap, Grae looked back into the box. Under the tissue paper, she found an envelope. Inside she found a yellowed piece of paper with deep creases where it had once been folded. Her vision blurred as she realized it was her own handwriting on the paper. It was the letter signed "Arabella Young".

"To whomever may one day find this letter: I was in the barn of Joseph Baker's, the evening of his death, on May 6, 1786. Although history may tell a different story, I know the truth. I saw the truth. It is almost too amazing for many to grasp. The ax that killed Joseph Baker was aimed by Sam at Isaiah. Sam was trying to defend me. Isaiah had a gun aimed at my head. When Sam heard a gunshot, he thought Isaiah had shot me. Isaiah was standing behind Joseph Baker, who was kneeling on the floor with his hands tied behind him.

Sam heard the shot and aimed the ax for Isaiah, but the shot had not come from Isaiah's gun. It came from a gun used by Patrick McGavock, who was also trying to protect me. Patrick shot Isaiah. Isaiah fell to the floor as the ax came down and split Joseph Baker's skull. It was an accident. Sam never intended to kill Joseph Baker, and Bob was off in the corner dazed and bleeding from an earlier fight with Isaiah.

You see, I am the one responsible for Joseph Baker's death. I did not deliver the blow, but I am responsible nonetheless. I shall carry this burden the rest of my days. Arabella Young."

A river of emotion once again washed over Grae. In her heart, she felt the words were true and now she knew that she was right. Underneath her signature was one sentence in a handwriting she did not know.

"Arabella speaks the truth. I was there. I saw it. But it is not her burden to bear. Nannie Baker."

For a long moment the air was still around Grae. She found that her breathing had slowed and she was deep, deep in thought.

"It was not my fault," she said out loud, "but that still doesn't mean that my presence was not felt."

Grae couldn't imagine a better birthday present. She couldn't dream that the week could have included any more adventure.

Her mother didn't ask what was in the box as Grae passed her on her way upstairs. Grae wanted her to see it, but not tonight. She set the box on the stairs, turned, and looked directly into her mother's eyes and hugged her. "Thanks, Mom. It was a very special day. I love you very much."

"You're all grown up now. I don't think I can bear it." There were tears in Kat's eyes, so many that the lines that framed them could not hold them all.

"I'll always be your little girl, Mom."

TWENTY SEVEN

Between school and the flurry of preparation for After Prom, Grae barely saw her mother on Thursday. But Friday was Senior Skip Day, and Grae knew it was time for her and her mother to have a long talk. Grandpa Mack took Perry to school and none of the committee was due to arrive for final decorations until the afternoon.

After a bite of breakfast, watching her mother with her many lists for the day, Grae decided that the time was now.

"I want to show you my dress."

"Oh, that's wonderful. I almost forgot about this mystery dress. I don't think I even know where you got it."

Grae took her mother upstairs, and Kat sat down on the bed watching as Grae took it out of the closet and unzipped the bag. It was a shock to Grae herself as she opened the bag. The colors of the dress were richer and more vibrant than she remembered. The stitching was more intricate. The bows danced lightly at the bottom as the dress moved. Grae noticed that a note was pinned to the outside of the bag. She'd thought it was just the bill when she picked it up. It said, "We hope you like how it turned out. It really amazed us. We tried to be very careful as we knew it was very old, but certainly it couldn't be as old as the tag indicates." Grae looked inside at the collar and saw a tag with the initials N.B. & M.B. and 1786. "After we cleaned it, the colors just came to life. It reminded us of *The Wizard of Oz*, when Dorothy steps out of the farmhouse into Oz and everything goes from dull black and white to vibrant color. It was like magic."

"My goodness, the dress looks like it is from another time." Kat took the dress out of Grae's hand and turned it all around, examining the workmanship.

"It is indeed."

Kat smiled and laughed a little, but then noticed that Grae's face was very serious. There was no joking on her face.

"Did you find it in one of the closets while you were cleaning?"

"No, but a closet is part of my story."

Kat continued to examine her daughter's face, searching for clues as to what she was talking about. "What about your hair? You never told me what made you decide to cut it."

"I didn't cut my hair."

"Oh, yes, well what made you decide to let Lucy cut off all those beautiful long strands? I wish you would have saved them." Kat walked toward the window.

"Lucy didn't cut my long hair. She only trimmed it up. It wasn't cut on Sunday, it happened two hundred years ago."

Kat whirled around. "What? What are you talking about?"

"You know what I am talking about. You've done it yourself."

As the wheels began to turn in Kat's mind, a look of fear crossed her face. She shook her head over and over again. "No, it's not possible. You don't know how. You couldn't have. It's over. It ended with me."

"I can't tell you the whole story now; we don't have time." Grae pulled her mother down and they sat on the bed. "I am okay and I didn't break any of the rules."

Kat's eyes filled with tears as she realized what Grae was saying to her. She took hold of Grae's right wrist and turned it over. Seeing the infinity symbol, Kat let out a small cry, a painful sound.

"Oh my, I'm so sorry, I should have prepared you, I should have warned you. I had no idea it could happen again. I thought I had done everything to prevent it."

Grae hugged her mother and let her cry. "We can't deny our destiny. We can't deny who we are. We can't deny our gift. There's a purpose behind it."

"You must have been terrified. How did you know what to do?"

"This will sound so silly, but I had a friend with me. It's all so strange, but The General, you know Grandpa's cat, he was with me and he told me what to do. I know, a talking cat, I must be delusional, but he did. He helped me find my way. He saved my life."

Grae didn't want to tell her mother the whole story yet. It would be too much for her to take in. There would be time later. Time for Kat to know the truth. Time for Grae to ask her questions. For now it was enough.

TWENTY EIGHT

Gav and Carrie arrived at five o'clock to pick up Grae and Perry. Grae's purple gown looked wonderful with Carrie's red hair and her mother had proven to be a very fast seamstress to make the necessary alterations. Perry looked sharp in his black tuxedo with purple bow tie and cummerbund.

Kat watched Grae walk down the staircase and caught her breath at how beautiful her daughter looked. It truly seemed as if she had stepped out of another time. Kat marveled at her daughter's resilience. How she could have endured what Kat knew was a terrifying adventure in another time, and a few days later, go off to a normal prom. It was the power of youth.

Stepping out onto the porch to stand next to her father, Kat then focused her eyes on the face of Gav McGavock. As he first viewed Grae in the doorway, Kat swore she saw a glow consume his face that could only be called love. She realized that this would not be a temporary romance. Come what may, Gav would be around for a while.

What Grae saw could only be described as déjà vu. She was back in 1786 and saw the face of Patrick before her, a tuxedo replaced by a dress coat with a long row of shiny brass buttons, and a stiff white shirt buttoned at the neck with a long, thin tie looped in a loose bow. As her vision cleared and she returned to her time, she again saw the handsome jock who had singled her out all those weeks ago in the cafeteria. The boy who had nervously asked her to the prom in his white grocery store apron; a young man whose feelings for her she knew had transcended time.

"You look simply, beautiful. I must bow to you." Patrick was still in there. It was a wonderful combination.

After all the photos were taken and the four of them left, Kat gazed out on the horizon, the mountains, the hills, and the valleys surrounding Graham Mansion. Her daughter had returned home, seemingly unharmed. But even without knowing Grae's story, Kat knew differently. Grae's life would never be the same. There would now be an edge to her daily existence. There was a ledge of time from which she might fall off. Then Kat saw the cat, The General, her father's pet, walking near a row of trees to the south. It stopped and looked toward her, as if it knew it was being watched. Could this animal have truly been Grae's saving grace? If it indeed was, who was it really, and how did it know so much about their family?

No one knew quite what to think about the newest senior. This was a girl whose father was in prison and she lived in SpookyWorld. Her dress turned everyone's head. Her hair was magical. There was an aura around her that made her appear as if she was floating the entire night, especially when she was in the arms of Gav. Every moment that they had that evening was a memory within itself. Even watching Carrie and Perry on the dance floor as the two of them, first awkwardly, learned how to dance together. It was hilarious and sweet at the same time.

There had been many special songs. The band had performed music from the previous three decades, especially the love songs that each generation of teens adored. As the evening drew to a close, one of the final songs was a Cher hit from the 80s, *If I Could Turn Back Time.* Grae laughed softly and gazed into Gav's eyes and smiled.

"I have a confession to make," Gav said.

"Oh, what's that?"

"The moment I first saw you, it was like I had known you before. It was crazy. I knew that you had just moved here. We had never met. But, somehow, you were so familiar," Gav laughed, "like I knew you in another life."

"Well, maybe you did."

"Yeah, right, you don't believe in all that do you? Carrothead's ramblings haven't rubbed off on you, have they?"

"Oh, I don't know. Anything is possible." Grae paused as they left the dance floor and walked through an open door. Standing in the moonlight, she continued. "I do know that you never know what might happen to you; where life may take you. A friend and an enemy can look very similar; so you have to listen to the truth that your heart tells you. You have to be ready to experience whatever comes your way and find the truth in it."

"Well, what is about to come your way is a kiss, Grae Belle."

Grae laughed, "Where did you hear that?"

"Your Grandpa said that was his pet name for you and that if I truly cared about you, I could use it, too."

"Well, let's not waste this moonlight, Mr. McGavock." As Gav and Grae kissed they felt the shimmer of the silver tips of her hair and she thinks to herself, "Thank you, Mr. Moon."

Carrie was ecstatic at how the Mansion decorations had come together. It was like a mini SpookyWorld with the feel of 19th century nobility. The food was delicious and elegant, but zombie-like at the same time. The music was ancient and modern simultaneously. She had convinced all of the seniors to stay in their prom attire for the beginning of the night. Kat and the committee had worked on many ideas for characters for the juniors to dress up as. Some came as historical figures from the Mansion's history, such as Squire David Graham and his wife, Martha. There were also more widely known characters. Elvis could be found in a jumpsuit in the parlor playing the piano. A zombie-like Paul Revere kept running around outside yelling, "The British are coming!" Even Abraham Lincoln was seen, looking as if he had received more than his share of bullets. Grae was amazed at all the thought that some of the kids had put into their costumes. The activities spilled out of the mansion into the yard and the barn with tents and white lights everywhere. The band lit up the stage and everyone danced in front of it.

Grae knew her mother could pull off some great parties, but she never realized that she could take a theme like this one and still make it classy and elegant. She really needed to convince her mother to go into business. This was truly her calling.

While Gav went to get them some drinks, Grae had a few minutes alone to reflect on everything that had happened. At first seeing all of the gruesome looks that some of the kids were costumed in made her flinch and have flashbacks. But as the night progressed, she began to relax and enjoy herself. She began to feel like a teenager again.

She smiled in amusement as she watched Gav walking toward her with Keith, a junior who was on Gav's baseball team. His costume could have been hand created by Carrie, it really looked authentic with a massive, gory latex head wound, blood soaked shirt, slowly walking, and carrying an axe.

Gav handed her the drink. The band was playing a loud song and the crowd of dancers were jumping up and down.

Grae turned to Keith, shouting, "So, who are you supposed to be, an axe murderer?"

Keith leaned toward her and whispered, "I'm the ghost of Joseph Baker."

Grae froze. The small knife in the secret pocket near the hem of her dress started moving and gave her a sudden jolt. Her vision began to blur and everything went black.

Historical Timeline

1745: William Mack, Seventh Day Adventist and "Drunkard," Max Meadows, Virginia, namesake, is the first settler on Reed Creek, west of the New River.

1747: Joseph Joel Baker is born to German immigrant parents in the Shenandoah Valley.

1756: Discovery of lead and iron ore by Colonel Chiswell; later known as Lead Mines; present day Austinville, Virginia.

1760: Fort Chiswell built; town of Lead Mines established.

1767: The first of six children. is born to Joseph and Nannie Baker; Baker serves in the militia which pays him through a land grant. Baker's home, farm, and distillery are located on present day Graham Mansion property.

1770: Botetourt County (western Virginia) formed from Augusta County.

1772: Fincastle County formed; Lead Mines serves as the county seat.

1774: Robert Graham, Squire David Graham's father, immigrates to America with his wife and four children from County Down, Ireland; serves in Revolutionary War. Squire David Graham is the Graham Mansion patriarch.

1775: Fincastle Resolutions signed in Lead Mines. Joseph Joel Baker serves in Revolutionary War.

1775-1800: 300,000 settlers traveled the Great Wagon Road through Fort Chiswell en route to the Cumberland Gap and beyond.

1776: Montgomery County formed; the Revolutionary War continues.

1782: Robert Graham's large family settles on Reed Creek at Locust Hill (present day Max Meadows, Virginia).

May 6, 1786: Joseph Joel Baker is murdered by his slaves, Bob and Sam. The sheriff is paid with 200 pounds of tobacco for capturing Bob and Sam, who are thus tried and convicted at the Lead Mines courthouse, and are subsequently hung.

1790: Wythe County formed.

September 3, 1800: Squire David Graham is born to Robert and Mary Cowen Graham at Locust Hill.

ABOUT THE AUTHORS

Rosa Lee Jude began creating her own imaginary worlds at an early age. While her career path has included stints in journalism, marketing, tourism and local government, she is most at home at a keyboard spinning yarns of fiction and creative non-fiction. She lives in the beautiful mountains of Southwest Virginia with her patient husband and very spoiled rescue dog. Visit her website at www.RosaLeeJude.com.

Mary Lin Brewer is a Carolina Tar Heel by birth, speech pathologist and school administrator by trade, and the mother of two miraculously stable offspring now in their twenties. A repressed history buff and late-bloomer to all things ghostly, Mary Lin is the official voice of the historical and haunted Major Graham Mansion. She resides in Dunedin, Florida and Wythe County, Virginia. Visit her website at www.MajorGrahamMansion.com.

To learn more about future books in this series, visit the upcoming website www.LegendsofGrahamMansion.com.